PENGUIN BOOKS

THE ROOM ON THE ROOF

RUSKIN BOND's first novel, *The Room on the Roof*, written when he was just seventeen, received the John Llewellyn Rhys Memorial Prize in 1957. Since then he has written a number of novellas, essays, poems and children's books. He has also written over five hundred short stories and articles that have appeared in magazines and anthologies. Ruskin Bond was born in Kasauli, Himachal Pradesh, and grew up in Jamnagar, Dehradun, New Delhi and Simla. As a young man, he spent four years in the Channel Islands and London. He returned to India in 1955. He now lives in Landour, Mussoorie, with his adopted family.

THE ROOM ON THE ROOF

Ruskin Bond

PENGUIN BOOKS

PENGUIN BOOKS

UK | USA | Canada | Ireland | Australia
India | New Zealand | South Africa

Penguin Books is part of the Penguin Random House group of companies
whose addresses can be found at global.penguinrandomhouse.com.

www.penguin.co.uk
www.puffin.co.uk
www.ladybird.co.uk

First published by Penguin Books India 1987
Published by Puffin Books India 2008
This edition published by Penguin Books 2017

001

Copyright © Ruskin Bond, 1987

The moral right of the author has been asserted

Set in 12.2/18 pt Dante MT Std
Typeset by Jouve (UK), Milton Keynes
Printed in Great Britain by Clays Ltd, St Ives plc

A CIP catalogue record for this book is available from the British Library

ISBN: 978–0–141–38676–8

All correspondence to:
Penguin Books
Penguin Random House Children's
80 Strand, London WC2R ORL

Introduction

Dear old room on the roof, I can't say I miss it (it was horribly hot at times), but I feel a certain nostalgia for that little *barsati* where I spent an important year of my life. It has long since vanished, the building having been pulled down to make way for something bigger and more impressive; but I am happy to report that the room still exists in this, my first novel, which has been around for sixty years, much to my own surprise and delight.

It had its genesis in 1951, the year after I finished school. I was waiting for a passage to England, making a little pocket money by writing stories for Indian magazines, and keeping a journal in which I wrote about my friends, neighbours, our little picnics and expeditions, and my hopes and dreams for the future. In due course this little *barsati* in Dehradun was exchanged for a small attic room in a London lodging house, and it was there, out of a longing for all that I'd left behind in India, that I turned my journal into a novel and called it *The Room on the Roof*.

It went the rounds of several publishers before it found a sympathetic editor in the person of Diana Athill, then a junior partner in the firm of André Deutsch. Diana went on to become a successful writer and a celebrity in her own right, but when I met her she was an editor, just a few years older than me. She showed my manuscript to Walter Allen, the well-known critic, and to Laurie Lee, the author, both of whom made encouraging sounds but advised against publishing the book, saying it would be a gamble.

But in those days publishers occasionally took gambles, and André Deutsch gave me a contract and an advance of £50. This was the standard advance in 1953.

However, it was two years before the book came out, and by that time I was back in India!

The Room on the Roof received favourable reviews; went into a German edition; received the John Llewellyn Rhys Prize (another £50), which was won by V. S. Naipaul a year later. But sales were poor, and the publishers shied away from doing another book of mine. Many years were to pass before another would be published in England, and then it would be not one but several books for children.

The Room on the Roof hadn't disappeared completely, and when in 1987 Penguin India brought out a new edition, it took off almost immediately, and over the last thirty years its readership has increased tremendously. It is never out of print, and it has far more readers today than when it was first published.

What makes it 'different', I think, is that it is a novel about adolescence by an adolescent; and for this reason I have never changed a word or made any revisions. It reflects the writer as he was when he wrote it – naive, trustful, eager for love and friendship. It was born out of the loneliness I felt as a young man on his own in a big city. I would work in an office all day, then return to my little bed-sitting room, slip a sheet of paper into my typewriter, and try to recapture the sights and sounds, the faces, the gestures, the spoken words, the important moments, the atmosphere, of all that I'd left behind.

Yes, it was written out of the loneliness of a young person longing for love and family. It has the passion and intensity we possess only when we are in our teens, and that, I think, is what has kept it alive all these years.

Landour, Mussoorie
August 2014   Ruskin Bond

Chapter One

The light spring rain rode on the wind, into the trees, down the road; it brought an exhilarating freshness to the air, a smell of earth, a scent of flowers; it brought a smile to the eyes of the boy on the road.

The long road wound round the hills, rose and fell and twisted down to Dehra; the road came from the mountains and passed through the jungle and valley and, after passing through Dehra, ended somewhere in the bazaar. But just where it ended no one knew, for the bazaar was a baffling place, where roads were easily lost.

The boy was three miles out of Dehra. The further he could get from Dehra, the happier he was likely to be. Just now he was only three miles out of Dehra, so he was not very happy; and, what was worse, he was walking homewards.

He was a pale boy, with blue-grey eyes and fair hair; his face was rough and marked, and the lower lip hung loose and heavy. He had his hands in his pockets and his head down, which was the way he always walked, and which gave him a deceptively tired appearance. He was a lazy but not a tired person.

He liked the rain as it flecked his face, he liked the smell and the freshness; he did not look at his surroundings or notice them – his mind, as usual, was very far away – but he felt their atmosphere, and he smiled.

His mind was so very far away that it was a few minutes before he noticed the swish of bicycle wheels beside him. The cyclist did not pass the boy, but rode beside him, studying him, taking in every visible detail, the bare head, the open-necked shirt, the flannel trousers, the sandals, the thick hide belt round his waist. A European boy was no longer a common sight in Dehra, and Somi, the cyclist, was interested.

'Hullo,' said Somi, 'would you like me to ride you into town? If you are going to town?'

'No, I'm all right,' said the boy, without slackening his pace, 'I like to walk.'

'So do I, but it's raining.'

And to support Somi's argument, the rain fell harder.

'I like to walk in the rain,' said the boy. 'And I don't live in the town, I live outside it.'

Nice people didn't live *in* the town . . .

'Well, I can pass your way,' persisted Somi, determined to help the stranger.

The boy looked again at Somi, who was dressed like him except for short pants and turban. Somi's legs were long and athletic, his colour was an unusually rich gold, his features were fine, his mouth broke easily into friendliness. It was impossible to resist the warmth of his nature.

The boy pulled himself up on the crossbar, in front of Somi, and they moved off.

They rode slowly, gliding round the low hills, and soon the jungle on either side of the road began to give way to open fields and tea gardens and then to orchards and one or two houses.

'Tell me when you reach your place,' said Somi. 'You stay with your parents?'

The boy considered the question too familiar for a stranger to ask and made no reply.

'Do you like Dehra?' asked Somi.

'Not much,' said the boy with pleasure.

'Well, after England it must seem dull . . .'

There was a pause and then the boy said: 'I haven't been to England. I was born here. I've never been anywhere else except Delhi.'

'Do you like Delhi?'

'Not much.'

They rode on in silence. The rain still fell, but the cycle moved smoothly over the wet road, making a soft, swishing sound.

Presently a man came in sight – no, it was not a man, it was a youth, but he had the appearance, the build of a man – walking towards town.

'Hey, Ranbir,' shouted Somi, as they neared the burly figure, 'want a lift?'

Ranbir ran into the road and slipped on to the carrier, behind Somi. The cycle wobbled a bit, but soon controlled itself and moved on, a little faster now.

Somi spoke into the boy's ear: 'Meet my friend Ranbir. He is the best wrestler in the bazaar.'

'Hullo, mister,' said Ranbir, before the boy could open his mouth.

'Hullo, mister,' said the boy.

Then Ranbir and Somi began a swift conversation in Punjabi, and the boy felt very lost; even, for some strange reason, jealous of the newcomer.

Now someone was standing in the middle of the road, frantically waving his arms and shouting incomprehensibly.

'It is Suri,' said Somi.

It was Suri.

Bespectacled and owlish to behold, Suri possessed an almost criminal cunning, and was both respected and despised by all who knew him. It was strange to find him out of town, for his interests were confined to people and their privacies; which privacies, when known to Suri, were soon made public.

He was a pale, bony, sickly boy, but he would probably live longer than Ranbir.

'Hey, give me a lift!' he shouted.

'Too many already,' said Somi.

'Oh, come on, Somi, I'm nearly drowned.'

'It's stopped raining.'

'Oh, come on . . .'

So Suri climbed on to the handlebar, which rather obscured Somi's view of the road and caused the cycle to wobble all over the place. Ranbir kept slipping on and off the carrier, and the boy found the crossbar exceedingly uncomfortable. The cycle had barely been controlled when Suri started to complain.

'It hurts,' he whimpered.

'I haven't got a cushion,' said Somi.

'It is a cycle,' said Ranbir bitingly, 'not a Rolls-Royce.'

Suddenly the road fell steeply, and the cycle gathered speed. 'Take it easy, now,' said Suri, 'or I'll fly off!'

'Hold tight,' warned Somi. 'It's downhill nearly all the way. We will have to go fast because the brakes aren't very good.'

'Oh, Mummy!' wailed Suri.

'Shut up!' said Ranbir.

The wind hit them with a sudden force, and their clothes blew up like balloons, almost tearing them from the machine. The boy forgot his discomfort and clung desperately to the crossbar, too nervous to say a word. Suri howled and Ranbir kept telling him to shut up, but Somi was enjoying the ride. He laughed merrily, a clear, ringing laugh, a laugh that bore no malice and no derision but only enjoyment, fun . . .

'It's all right for you to laugh,' said Suri. 'If anything happens, *I'll* get hurt!'

'If anything happens,' said Somi, 'we *all* get hurt!'

'That's right,' shouted Ranbir from behind.

The boy closed his eyes and put his trust in God and Somi – but mainly Somi . . .

'Oh, Mummy!' wailed Suri.

'Shut up!' said Ranbir.

The road twisted and turned as much as it could, and rose a little only to fall more steeply the other side. But eventually it began to even out, for they were nearing the town and almost in the residential area.

'The run is over,' said Somi, a little regretfully.

'Oh, Mummy!'

'Shut up.'

The boy said: 'I must get off now, I live very near.'

Somi skidded the cycle to a standstill, and Suri shot off the handlebar into a muddy sidetrack. The boy slipped off, but Somi and Ranbir remained on their seats, Ranbir steadying the cycle with his feet on the ground.

'Well, thank you,' said the boy.

Somi said: 'Why don't you come and have your meal with us? There is not much further to go.'

The boy's shyness would not fall away.

'I've got to go home,' he said. 'I'm expected. Thanks very much.'

'Well, come and see us some time,' said Somi. 'If you come to the chaat shop in the bazaar, you are sure to find one of us. You know the bazaar?'

'Well, I have passed through it – in a car.'

'Oh.'

The boy began walking away, his hands once more in his pockets.

'Hey!' shouted Somi. 'You didn't tell us your name!'

The boy turned and hesitated and then said, 'Rusty . . .'

'See you soon, Rusty,' said Somi, and the cycle pushed off.

The boy watched the cycle receding down the road, and Suri's shrill voice came to him on the wind. It had stopped raining, but the boy was unaware of this; he was almost home, and that was a miserable thought. To his surprise and disgust, he found himself wishing he had gone into Dehra with Somi.

He stood in the sidetrack and stared down the empty road; and, to his surprise and disgust, he felt immeasurably lonely.

Chapter Two

When a large white butterfly settled on the missionary's wife's palatial bosom, she felt flattered, and allowed it to remain there. Her garden was beginning to burst into flower, giving her great pleasure – her husband gave her none – and such fellow-feeling as to make her tread gingerly among the caterpillars.

Mr John Harrison, the boy's guardian, felt only contempt for the good lady's buoyancy of spirit, but nevertheless gave her an ingratiating smile.

'I hope you'll put the boy to work while I'm away,' he said. 'Make some use of him. He dreams too much. Most unfortunate that he's finished with school, I don't know what to do with him.'

'He doesn't know what to do with himself,' said the missionary's wife. 'But I'll keep him occupied. He can do some weeding, or read to me in the afternoon. I'll keep an eye on him.'

'Good,' said the guardian. And, having cleared his conscience, he made quick his escape.

Over lunch he told the boy: 'I'm going to Delhi tomorrow. Business.'

It was the only thing he said during the meal. When he had finished eating, he lit a cigarette and erected a curtain of smoke between himself and the boy. He was a heavy smoker, his fingers were stained a deep yellow.

'How long will you be gone, sir?' asked Rusty, trying to sound casual.

Mr Harrison did not reply. He seldom answered the boy's questions, and his own were stated, not asked; he probed and suggested, sharply, quickly, without ever encouraging loose conversation. He never talked about himself; he never argued: he would tolerate no argument.

He was a tall man, neat in appearance; and, though over forty, looked younger because he kept his hair short, shaving above the ears. He had a small ginger tooth-brush moustache.

Rusty was afraid of his guardian.

Mr Harrison, who was really a cousin of the boy's father, had done a lot for Rusty, and that was why the boy was afraid of him. Since his parents had died, Rusty had been kept, fed and paid for, and sent to an expensive school in the hills that was run on 'exclusively European lines'. He had, in a way, been bought by Mr Harrison. And now he was owned by him. And he must do as his guardian wished. Rusty was ready to do as his guardian wished: he had always obeyed him. But he was afraid of the man, afraid of his silence and of the ginger moustache and of the supple malacca cane that lay in the glass cupboard in the drawing room.

Lunch over, the boy left his guardian giving the cook orders and went to his room.

The window looked out on the garden path, and a sweeper boy moved up and down the path, a bucket clanging against his naked thighs. He wore only a loincloth, his body was bare and burnt a deep brown, and his head was shaved clean. He went to and from the water tank, and every time he returned to it he bathed, so that his body continually glistened with moisture.

Apart from Rusty, the only boy in the European community of Dehra was this sweeper boy, the low-caste untouchable, the cleaner of pots. But the two seldom spoke to each other, one was a servant and the other a sahib and anyway, muttered Rusty to himself, playing with the sweeper boy would be unhygienic . . .

The missionary's wife had said: 'Even if you were an Indian, my child, you would not be allowed to play with the sweeper boy.' So that Rusty often wondered: with whom, then, could the sweeper boy play?

The untouchable passed by the window and smiled, but Rusty looked away.

Over the tops of the cherry trees were mountains. Dehra lay in a valley in the foothills, and the small, diminishing European community had its abode on the outskirts of the town.

Mr John Harrison's house, and the other houses, were all built in an English style, with neat front gardens and nameplates on the gates. The surroundings on the whole were so English that the people often found it difficult to believe that they did live at the foot of the Himalayas, surrounded by India's thickest jungles. India started a mile away, where the bazaar began.

To Rusty, the bazaar sounded a fascinating place, and what he had seen of it from the window of his guardian's car had been enough to make his heart pound excitedly and his imagination soar; but it was a forbidden place – full of thieves and germs' said the missionary's wife – and the boy never entered it, save in his dreams.

For Mr Harrison, the missionaries, and their neighbours,

this country district of blossoming cherry trees was India. They knew there was a bazaar and a real India not far away, but they did not speak of such places, they chose not to think about them.

The community consisted mostly of elderly people; the others had left soon after independence. These few stayed because they were too old to start life again in another country, where there would be no servants and very little sunlight; and, though they complained of their lot and criticized the government, they knew their money could buy them their comforts: servants, good food, whisky, almost anything – except the dignity they cherished most . . .

But the boy's guardian, though he enjoyed the same comforts, remained in the country for different reasons. He did not care who were the rulers so long as they didn't take away his business; he had shares in a number of small tea estates and owned some land – forested land – where, for instance, he hunted deer and wild pig.

Rusty, being the only young person in the community, was the centre of everyone's attention, particularly the ladies'.

He was also very lonely.

Every day he walked aimlessly along the road, over the

hillside; brooding on the future, or dreaming of sudden and perfect companionship, romance and heroics; hardly ever conscious of the present. When an opportunity for friendship did present itself, as it had the previous day, he shied away, preferring his own company.

His idle hours were crowded with memories, snatches of childhood. He could not remember what his parents were like, but in his mind there were pictures of sandy beaches covered with seashells of every description. They had lived on the west coast, in the Gulf of Kutch; there had been a gramophone that played records of Gracie Fields and Harry Lauder, and a captain of a cargo ship who gave the child bars of chocolate and piles of comics – *The Dandy, Beano, Tiger Tim* – and spoke of the wonderful countries he had visited. But the boy's guardian seldom spoke of Rusty's childhood, or his parents, and this secrecy lent mystery to the vague, undefined memories that hovered in the boy's mind like hesitant ghosts.

Rusty spent much of his time studying himself in the dressing table mirror; he was able to ignore his pimples and see a grown man, worldly and attractive. Though only sixteen, he felt much older.

He was white. His guardian was pink, and the missionary's wife a bright red, but Rusty was white. With his thick lower lip and prominent cheekbones, he looked slightly Mongolian, especially in a half-light. He often wondered why no one else in the community had the same features.

Mr John Harrison was going to Delhi.

Rusty intended making the most of his guardian's absence: he would squeeze all the freedom he could out of the next few days; explore, get lost, wander afar; even if it were only to find new places to dream in. So he threw himself on the bed and visualized the morrow . . . where should he go – into the hills again, into the forest? Or should he listen to the devil in his heart and go into the bazaar? Tomorrow he would know, tomorrow . . .

Chapter Three

It was a cold morning, sharp and fresh. It was quiet until the sun came shooting over the hills, lifting the mist from the valley and clearing the blood-shot from the sky. The ground was wet with dew.

On the maidan, a broad stretch of grassland, Ranbir and another youth wrestled each other, their muscles rippling, their well-oiled limbs catching the first rays of the sun as it climbed the horizon. Somi sat on his veranda steps; his long hair loose, resting on his knees, drying in the morning sun. Suri was still dead to the world, lost in blanket; he cared not for the morning or the sun.

Rusty stood at the gate until his guardian was comfortably seated behind the wheel of the car, and did not move until it had disappeared round the bend in the road.

The missionary's wife, that large cauliflower-like lady, rose unexpectedly from behind a hedge and called: 'Good morning, dear! If you aren't very busy this morning, would you like to give me a hand pruning this hedge?'

The missionary's wife was fond of putting Rusty to work in her garden: if it wasn't cutting the hedge, it was weeding the flower beds and watering the plants, or clearing the garden path of stones, or hunting beetles and ladybirds and dropping them over the wall.

'Oh, good morning,' stammered Rusty. 'Actually, I was going for a walk. Can I help you when I come back, I won't be long . . .'

The missionary's wife was rather taken aback, for Rusty seldom said no; and before she could make another sally the boy was on his way. He had a dreadful feeling she would call him back; she was a kind woman, but talkative and boring, and Rusty knew what would follow the garden work: weak tea or lemonade, and then a game of cards, probably beggar-my-neighbour.

But to his relief she called after him: 'All right, dear, come back soon. And be good!'

He waved to her and walked rapidly down the road. And the direction he took was different to the one in which he usually wandered.

Far down this road was the bazaar. First Rusty must pass the rows of neat cottages, arriving at a commercial area – Dehra's Westernized shopping centre – where Europeans, rich Indians, and American tourists *en route* for Mussoorie, could eat at smart restaurants and drink prohibited alcohol. But the boy was afraid and distrustful of anything smart and sophisticated, and he hurried past the shopping centre.

He came to the Clock Tower, which was a tower without a clock. It had been built from public subscriptions but not enough money had been gathered for the addition of a clock. It had been lifeless five years but served as a good landmark. On the other side of the Clock Tower lay the bazaar, and in the bazaar lay India. On the other side of the Clock Tower began life itself. And all three – the bazaar and India and life itself – were forbidden.

Rusty's heart was beating fast as he reached the Clock Tower. He was about to defy the law of his guardian and of his community. He stood at the Clock Tower, nervous, hesitant, biting his nails. He was afraid of discovery and punishment, but hungering curiosity impelled him forward.

The bazaar and India and life itself all began with a rush of noise and confusion.

The boy plunged into the throng of bustling people; the road was hot and close, alive with the cries of vendors and the smell of cattle and ripening dung. Children played hopscotch in alleyways or gambled with coins, scuffling in the gutter for a lost anna. And the cows moved leisurely through the crowd, nosing around for paper and stale, discarded vegetables; the more daring cows helping themselves at open stalls. And above the uneven tempo of the noise came the blare of a loudspeaker playing a popular piece of music.

Rusty moved along with the crowd, fascinated by the sight of beggars lying on the roadside: naked and emaciated half-humans, some skeletons, some covered with sores; old men dying, children dying, mothers with sucking babies, living and dying. But, strangely enough, the boy could feel nothing for these people; perhaps it was because they were no longer recognizable as humans or because he could not see himself in the same circumstances. And no one else in the bazaar seemed to feel for them. Like the cows and the loudspeaker, the beggars were a natural growth in the bazaar, and only the well-to-do – sacrificing a few annas to placate their consciences – were aware of the beggars' presence.

Every little shop was different from the one next to it. After the vegetable stand, green and wet, came the fruit stall; and after the fruit stall, the tea and betel-leaf shop;

then the astrologer's platform (Manmohan Mukuldev, B.Astr., foreign degree); and after the astrologer's, the toy shop, selling trinkets of gay colours. And then, after the toy shop, another from whose doors poured clouds of smoke.

Out of curiosity Rusty turned to the shop from which the smoke was coming. But he was not the only person making for it. Approaching from the opposite direction was Somi on his bicycle.

Somi, who had not seen Rusty, seemed determined on riding right into the smoky shop on his bicycle; unfortunately his way was blocked by Maharani, the queen of the bazaar cows, who moved aside for no one. But the cycle did not lose speed.

Rusty, seeing the cycle but not recognizing the rider, felt sorry for the cow; it was sure to be hurt. But, with the devil in his heart or in the wheels of his machine, Somi swung clear of Maharani and collided with Rusty and knocked him into the gutter.

Accustomed as Rusty was to the delicate scents of the missionary's wife's sweet peas and the occasional smell of bathroom disinfectant, he was nevertheless overpowered by the odour of bad vegetables and kitchen water that rose from the gutter.

'What the hell do you think you're doing?' he cried, choking and spluttering.

'Hullo,' said Somi, gripping Rusty by the arm and helping him up, 'so sorry, not my fault. Anyway, we meet again!'

Rusty felt for injuries and, finding none, exclaimed: 'Look at the filthy mess I'm in!'

Somi could not help laughing at the other's unhappy condition. 'Oh, that is not filth, it is only cabbage water! Do not worry, the clothes will dry . . .'

His laugh rang out merrily, and there was something about the laugh, some music in it perhaps, that touched a chord of gaiety in Rusty's own heart. Somi was smiling, and on his mouth the smile was friendly and in his soft brown eyes it was mocking.

'Well, I am sorry,' said Somi, extending his hand.

Rusty did not take the hand but, looking the other up and down, from turban to slippers, forced himself to say: 'Get out of my way, please.'

'You are a snob,' said Somi without moving. 'You are a very funny one too.'

'I am not a snob,' said Rusty involuntarily.

'Then why not forget an accident?'

'You could have missed me, but you didn't try.'

'But if I had missed you, I would have hit the cow! You don't know Maharani; if you hurt her she goes mad and smashes half the bazaar! Also, the bicycle might have been spoilt . . . Now please come and have chaat with me.'

Rusty had no idea what was meant by the word chaat, but before he could refuse the invitation Somi had bundled him into the shop from which the smoke still poured.

At first nothing could be made out; then gradually the smoke seemed to clear and there in front of the boys, like some shining god, sat a man enveloped in rolls of glistening, oily flesh. In front of him, on a coal fire, was a massive pan in which sizzled a sea of fat; and with deft, practised fingers, he moulded and flipped potato cakes in and out of the pan.

The shop was crowded; but so thick was the screen of smoke and steam, that it was only the murmur of conversation which made known the presence of many people. A plate made of banana leaves was thrust into Rusty's hands, and two fried cakes suddenly appeared in it.

'Eat!' said Somi, pressing the novice down until they were both seated on the floor, their backs to the wall.

'They are tikkees,' explained Somi, 'tell me if you like them.'

Rusty tasted a bit. It was hot. He waited a minute, then tasted another bit. It was still hot but in a different way; now it was lively, interesting; it had a different taste to anything he had eaten before. Suspicious but inquisitive, he finished the tikkee and waited to see if anything would happen.

'Have you had before?' asked Somi.

'No,' said Rusty anxiously, 'what will it do?'

'It might worry your stomach a little at first, but you will get used to it the more often you eat. So finish the other one too.'

Rusty had not realized the extent of his submission to the other's wishes. At one moment he had been angry, ill-mannered; but, since the laugh, he had obeyed Somi without demur.

Somi wore a cotton tunic and shorts, and sat cross-legged, his feet pressed against his thighs. His skin was a golden brown, dark on his legs and arms but fair, very fair, where his shirt lay open. His hands were dirty; but eloquent. His eyes, deep brown and dreamy, had depth and roundness.

He said: 'My name is Somi, please tell me what is yours, I have forgotten.'

'Rusty . . .'

'How do you do,' said Somi, 'I am very pleased to meet you, haven't we met before?'

Rusty mumbled to himself in an effort to sulk.

'That was a long time ago,' said Somi, 'now we are friends, yes, best favourite friends!'

Rusty continued to mumble under his breath, but he took the warm muddy hand that Somi gave him, and shook it. He finished the tikkee on his leaf, and accepted another. Then he said: 'How do you do, Somi, I am very pleased to meet you.'

Chapter Four

The missionary's wife's head projected itself over the garden wall and broke into a beam of welcome. Rusty hurriedly returned the smile.

'Where have you been, dear?' asked his garrulous neighbour. 'I was expecting you for lunch. You've never been away so long. I've finished all my work now, you know . . . Was it a nice walk? I know you're thirsty, come in and have a nice cool lemonade, there's nothing like iced lemonade to refresh one after a long walk. I remember when I was a girl, having to walk down to Dehra from Mussoorie, I filled my thermos with lemonade . . .'

But Rusty had gone. He did not wish to hurt the missionary's wife's feelings by refusing the lemonade but, after experiencing the chaat shop, the very idea of a lemonade offended him. But he decided that this Sunday he would contribute an extra four annas to the missionary's fund for upkeep of church, wife and garden; and, with this good thought in mind, went to his room.

The sweeper boy passed by the window, his buckets clanging, his feet going slip-slop on the watery path.

Rusty threw himself on his bed. And now his imagination began building dreams on a new-found reality, for he had agreed to meet Somi again.

And so, the next day, his steps took him to the chaat shop in the bazaar; past the Clock Tower, past the smart shops, down the road, far from the guardian's house.

The fleshy god of the tikkees smiled at Rusty in a manner that seemed to signify that the boy was now likely to become a regular customer. The banana plate was ready, the tikkees in it flavoured with spiced sauces.

'Hullo, best favourite friend,' said Somi, appearing out of the surrounding vapour, his slippers loose, *chup-chup-chup*; loose, open slippers that hung on to the toes by a strap and slapped against the heels as he walked. 'I am glad you come again. After tikkees you must have something else, chaat or gol guppas, all right?'

Somi removed his slippers and joined Rusty, who had somehow managed to sit cross-legged on the ground in the proper fashion.

Somi said, 'Tell me something about yourself. By what misfortune are you an Englishman? How is it that you have been here all your life and never been to a chaat shop before?'

'Well, my guardian is very strict,' said Rusty. 'He wanted to bring me up in English ways, and he has succeeded . . .'

'Till now,' said Somi, and laughed, the laugh rippling up in his throat, breaking out and forcing its way through the smoke.

Then a large figure loomed in front of the boys, and Rusty recognized him as Ranbir, the youth he had met on the bicycle.

'Another best favourite friend,' said Somi.

Ranbir did not smile, but opened his mouth a little, gaped at Rusty, and nodded his head. When he nodded, hair fell untidily across his forehead; thick black bushy hair, wild and uncontrollable. He wore a long white cotton tunic hanging out over his baggy pyjamas; his feet were bare and dirty; big feet, strong.

'Hullo, mister,' said Ranbir, in a gruff voice that disguised his shyness. He said no more for a while, but joined them in their meal. They ate chaat, a spicy salad of potato, guava and orange; and then gol guppas, baked flour-cups filled with burning syrups. Rusty felt at ease and began to talk, telling his companions about his school in the hills, the house of his guardian, Mr Harrison himself, and the supple malacca cane. The story was listened to with some amusement: apparently Rusty's life had been very dull to date, and Somi and Ranbir pitied him for it.

'Tomorrow is Holi,' said Ranbir, 'you must play with me, then you will be my friend.'

'What is Holi?' asked Rusty.

Ranbir looked at him in amazement. 'You do not know about Holi! It is the Hindu festival of colour! It is the day on which we celebrate the coming of spring, when we throw colour on each other and shout and sing and forget our misery, for the colours mean the rebirth of spring and a new life in our hearts . . . You do not know of it!'

Rusty was somewhat bewildered by Ranbir's sudden eloquence, and began to have doubts about this game; it seemed to him a primitive sort of pastime, this throwing of paint about the place.

'I might get into trouble,' he said. 'I'm not supposed to come here anyway, and my guardian might return any day . . .'

'Don't tell him about it,' said Ranbir.

'Oh, he has ways of finding out. I'll get a thrashing.'

'Huh!' said Ranbir, a disappointed and somewhat disgusted expression on his mobile face. 'You are afraid to spoil your clothes, mister, that is it. You are just a snob.'

Somi laughed. 'That's what I told him yesterday, and only then did he join me in the chaat shop. I think we should call him a snob whenever he makes excuses.'

Rusty was enjoying the chaat. He ate gol guppa after gol guppa, until his throat was almost aflame and his stomach burning itself out. He was not very concerned about Holi. He was content with the present, content to enjoy the new-found pleasures of the chaat shop, and said: 'Well, I'll see . . . If my guardian doesn't come back tomorrow, I'll play Holi with you, all right?'

Ranbir was pleased. He said, 'I will be waiting in the jungle behind your house. When you hear the drumbeat in the jungle, then it is me. Then come.'

'Will you be there too, Somi?' asked Rusty. Somehow, he felt safe in Somi's presence.

'I do not play Holi,' said Somi. 'You see, I am different to Ranbir. I wear a turban and he does not, also there is a bangle on my wrist, which means that I am a Sikh. We don't play it. But I will see you the day after, here in the chaat shop.'

Somi left the shop, and was swallowed up by smoke and steam, but the *chup-chup* of his loose slippers could be heard for some time, until their sound was lost in the greater sound of the bazaar outside.

In the bazaar, people haggled over counters, children played in the spring sunshine, dogs courted one another, and Ranbir and Rusty continued eating gol guppas.

The afternoon was warm and lazy, unusually so for spring; very quiet, as though resting in the interval between the spring and the coming summer. There was no sign of the missionary's wife or the sweeper boy when Rusty returned, but Mr Harrison's car stood in the driveway of the house.

At the sight of the car, Rusty felt a little weak and frightened; he had not expected his guardian to return so soon and had, in fact, almost forgotten his existence. But now he forgot all about the chaat shop and Somi and Ranbir, and ran up the veranda steps in a panic.

Mr Harrison was at the top of the veranda steps, standing behind the potted palms.

The boy said, 'Oh, hullo, sir, you're back!' He knew of nothing else to say, but tried to make his little piece sound enthusiastic.

'Where have you been all day?' asked Mr Harrison, without looking once at the startled boy. 'Our neighbours haven't seen much of you lately.'

'I've been for a walk, sir.'

'You have been to the bazaar.'

The boy hesitated before making a denial; the man's eyes were on him now, and to lie Rusty would have had to lower his eyes – and this he could not do . . .

'Yes, sir, I went to the bazaar.'

'May I ask why?'

'Because I had nothing to do.'

'If you had nothing to do, you could have visited our neighbours. The bazaar is not the place for you. You know that.'

'But nothing happened to me . . .'

'That is not the point,' said Mr Harrison, and now his normally dry voice took on a faint shrill note of excitement, and he spoke rapidly. 'The point is, I have told you never to visit the bazaar. You belong here, to this house, this road, these people. Don't go where you don't belong.'

Rusty wanted to argue, longed to rebel, but fear of Mr Harrison held him back. He wanted to resist the man's authority, but he was conscious of the supple malacca cane in the glass cupboard.

'I'm sorry, sir . . .'

But his cowardice did him no good. The guardian went over to the glass cupboard, brought out the cane, flexed it in his hands. He said, 'It is not enough to say you are sorry, you must be made to feel sorry. Bend over the sofa.'

The boy bent over the sofa, clenched his teeth and dug his fingers into the cushions. The cane swished through the air, landing on his bottom with a slap, knocking the dust from his pants. Rusty felt no pain. But his guardian waited, allowing the cut to sink in, then he administered the second stroke, and this time it hurt, it stung into the boy's buttocks, burning up the flesh, conditioning it for the remaining cuts.

At the sixth stroke of the supple malacca cane, which was usually the last, Rusty let out a wild whoop, leapt over the sofa and charged from the room.

He lay groaning on his bed until the pain had eased.

But the flesh was so sore that he could not touch the place where the cane had fallen. Wriggling out of his pants, he examined his backside in the mirror. Mr Harrison had been most accurate: a thick purple welt stretched across both cheeks, and a little blood trickled down the boy's thigh. The blood had a cool, almost soothing effect, but the sight of it made Rusty feel faint.

He lay down and moaned for pleasure. He pitied himself enough to want to cry, but he knew the futility of tears. But the pain and the sense of injustice he felt were both real.

A shadow fell across the bed. Someone was at the window, and Rusty looked up.

The sweeper boy showed his teeth.

'What do you want?' asked Rusty gruffly.

'You hurt, chotta sahib?'

The sweeper boy's sympathies provoked only suspicion in Rusty.

'You told Mr Harrison where I went!' said Rusty.

But the sweeper boy cocked his head to one side, and asked innocently, 'Where you went, chotta sahib?'

'Oh, never mind. Go away.'

'But you hurt?'

'Get out!' shouted Rusty.

The smile vanished, leaving only a sad, frightened look in the sweeper boy's eyes.

Rusty hated hurting people's feelings, but he was not accustomed to familiarity with servants; and yet, only a few minutes ago, he had been beaten for visiting the bazaar where there were so many like the sweeper boy.

The sweeper boy turned from the window, leaving wet fingermarks on the sill; then lifted his buckets from the ground and, with his knees bent to take the weight, walked away. His feet splashed a little in the water he had spilt, and the soft red mud flew up and flecked his legs.

Angry with his guardian and with the servant and most of all with himself, Rusty buried his head in his pillow and tried to shut out reality; he forced a dream, in which he was thrashing Mr Harrison until the guardian begged for mercy.

Chapter Five

In the early morning, when it was still dark, Ranbir stopped in the jungle behind Mr Harrison's house, and slapped his drum. His thick mass of hair was covered with red dust and his body, naked but for a cloth round his waist, was smeared green; he looked like a painted god, a green god. After a minute he slapped the drum again, then sat down on his heels and waited.

Rusty woke to the sound of the second drumbeat, and lay in bed and listened; it was repeated, travelling over the still air and in through the bedroom window. *Dhum!* . . . a double beat now, one deep, one high, insistent, questioning . . . Rusty remembered his promise, that he would play Holi with Ranbir, meet him in the jungle when he beat the drum. But he had made the promise on the condition that his guardian did not return; he could not possibly keep it now, not after the thrashing he had received.

Dhum-dhum, spoke the drum in the forest; *dhum-dhum*, impatient and getting annoyed . . .

'Why can't he shut up?' muttered Rusty. 'Does he want to wake Mr Harrison . . . ?'

Holi, the festival of colours, the arrival of spring, the rebirth of the new year, the awakening of love, what were these things to him? They did not concern his life, he could not start a new life, not for one day . . . and besides, it all sounded very primitive, this throwing of colour and beating of drums . . .

Dhum-dhum!

The boy sat up in bed.

The sky had grown lighter.

From the distant bazaar came a new music, many drums and voices, faint but steady, growing in rhythm and excitement. The sound conveyed something to Rusty, something wild and emotional, something that belonged to his dream world, and on a sudden impulse he sprang out of bed.

He went to the door and listened. The house was quiet; he bolted the door. The colours of Holi, he knew, would stain his clothes, so he did not remove his pyjamas. In an old pair of flattened rubber-soled tennis shoes, he climbed out of the window and ran over the dew-wet grass, down the path behind the house, over the hill and into the jungle.

When Ranbir saw the boy approach, he rose from the ground. The long hand-drum, the dholak, hung at his waist. As he rose, the sun rose. But the sun did not look as fiery as Ranbir who, in Rusty's eyes, appeared as a painted demon, rather than as a god.

'You are late, mister,' said Ranbir, 'I thought you were not coming.'

He had both his fists closed, but when he walked towards Rusty he opened them, smiling widely, a white smile in a green face. In his right hand was the red dust and in his left hand the green dust. And with his right hand he rubbed the red dust on Rusty's left cheek, and then with the other hand he put the green dust on the boy's right cheek; then he stood back and looked at Rusty and laughed. Then, according to the custom, he embraced the bewildered boy. It was a wrestler's hug, and Rusty winced breathlessly.

'Come,' said Ranbir, 'let us go and make the town a rainbow.'

And truly, that day there was an outbreak of spring.

The sun came up, and the bazaar woke up. The walls of the houses were suddenly patched with splashes of colour, and just as suddenly the trees seemed to have burst into flower; for in the forest there were armies of rhododendrons, and by the river the poinsettias danced; the cherry and the plum were in blossom; the snow in the mountains had melted, and the streams were rushing torrents; the new leaves on the trees were full of sweetness, and the young grass held both dew and sun, and made an emerald of every dewdrop.

The infection of spring spread simultaneously through the world of man and the world of nature, and made them one.

Ranbir and Rusty moved round the hill, keeping in the fringe of the jungle until they had skirted not only the European community but also the smart shopping centre. They came down dirty little side streets where the walls of houses, stained with the wear and tear of many years of meagre habitation, were now stained again with the vivid colours of Holi. They came to the Clock Tower.

At the Clock Tower, spring had really been declared open. Clouds of coloured dust rose in the air and spread, and jets of water – green and orange and purple, all rich, emotional colours – burst out everywhere.

Children formed groups. They were armed mainly with bicycle pumps, or pumps fashioned from bamboo stems, from which was squirted liquid colour. And the children paraded the main road, chanting shrilly and clapping their hands. The men and women preferred the dust to the water. They, too, sang, but their chanting held a significance, their hands and fingers drummed the rhythms of spring, the same rhythms, the same songs that belonged to this day every year of their lives.

Ranbir was met by some friends and greeted with great hilarity. A bicycle pump was directed at Rusty and a jet of sooty black water squirted into his face.

Blinded for a moment, Rusty blundered about in great confusion. A horde of children bore down on him, and he was subjected to a pumping from all sides. His shirt and pyjamas, drenched through, stuck to his skin; then someone gripped the end of his shirt and tugged at it until it tore and came away. Dust was thrown on the boy, on his face and body, roughly and with full force, and his tender, underexposed skin smarted beneath the onslaught.

Then his eyes cleared. He blinked and looked wildly round at the group of boys and girls who cheered and danced in front of him. His body was running mostly with sooty black, streaked with red, and his mouth seemed full of it too, and he began to spit.

Then, one by one, Ranbir's friends approached Rusty.

Gently, they rubbed dust on the boy's cheeks, and embraced him; they were so like many flaming demons that Rusty could not distinguish one from the other. But this gentle greeting, coming so soon after the stormy bicycle pump attack, bewildered Rusty even more.

Ranbir said: 'Now you are one of us, come,' and Rusty went with him and the others.

'Suri is hiding,' cried someone. 'He has locked himself in his house and won't play Holi!'

'Well, he will have to play,' said Ranbir, 'even if we break the house down.'

Suri, who dreaded Holi, had decided to spend the day in a state of siege; and had set up camp in his mother's kitchen, where there were provisions enough for the whole day. He listened to his playmates calling to him from the courtyard, and ignored their invitations, jeers, and threats; the door was strong and well barricaded. He settled himself beneath a table, and turned the pages of the English nudists' journal, which he bought every month chiefly for its photographic value.

But the youths outside, intoxicated by the drumming and shouting and high spirits, were not going to be done out of the pleasure of discomfiting Suri. So they acquired a ladder and made their entry into the kitchen by the skylight.

down the roads, out of the town and into the forest. And, for one day, Rusty forgot his guardian and the missionary's wife and the supple malacca cane, and ran with the others through the town and into the forest.

The crisp, sunny morning ripened into afternoon.

In the forest, in the cool dark silence of the jungle, they stopped singing and shouting, suddenly exhausted. They lay down in the shade of many trees, and the grass was soft and comfortable, and very soon everyone except Rusty was fast asleep.

Rusty was tired. He was hungry. He had lost his shirt and shoes, his feet were bruised, his body sore. It was only now, resting, that he noticed these things, for he had been caught up in the excitement of the colour game, overcome by an exhilaration he had never known. His fair hair was tousled and streaked with colour, and his eyes were wide with wonder.

He was exhausted now, but he was happy.

He wanted this to go on forever, this day of feverish emotion, this life in another world. He did not want to leave the forest; it was safe, its earth soothed him, gathered him in, so that the pain of his body became a pleasure . . .

He did not want to go home.

Suri squealed with fright. The door was opened and he was bundled out, and his spectacles were trampled.

'My glasses!' he screamed. 'You've broken them!'

'You can afford a dozen pairs!' jeered one of his antagonists.

'But I can't see, you fools, I can't see!'

'He can't see!' cried someone in scorn. 'For once in his life, Suri can't see what's going on! Now, whenever he spies, we'll smash his glasses!'

Not knowing Suri very well, Rusty could not help pitying the frantic boy.

'Why don't you let him go?' he asked Ranbir. 'Don't force him if he doesn't want to play.'

'But this is the only chance we have of repaying him for all his dirty tricks. It is the only day on which no one is afraid of him!'

Rusty could not imagine how anyone could possibly be afraid of the pale, struggling, spindly-legged boy who was almost being torn apart, and was glad when the others had finished their sport with him.

All day Rusty roamed the town and countryside with Ranbir and his friends, and Suri was soon forgotten. For one day, Ranbir and his friends forgot their homes and their work and the problem of the next meal, and danced

Chapter Six

Mr Harrison stood at the top of the veranda steps. The house was in darkness, but his cigarette glowed more brightly for it. A road lamp trapped the returning boy as he opened the gate, and Rusty knew he had been seen, but he didn't care much; if he had known that Mr Harrison had not recognized him, he would have turned back instead of walking resignedly up the garden path.

Mr Harrison did not move, nor did he appear to notice the boy's approach. It was only when Rusty climbed the veranda steps that his guardian moved and said: 'Who's that?'

Still he had not recognized the boy; and in that instant Rusty become aware of his own condition, for his body was a patchwork of paint. Wearing only torn pyjamas he could, in the half-light, have easily been mistaken for the sweeper boy or someone else's servant. It must have been a newly acquired bazaar instinct that made the boy think of escape. He turned about.

But Mr Harrison shouted, 'Come here, you!' and the tone of his voice – the tone reserved for the sweeper boy – made Rusty stop.

'Come up here!' repeated Mr Harrison.

Rusty returned to the veranda, and his guardian switched on a light; but even now there was no recognition.

'Good evening, sir,' said Rusty.

Mr Harrison received a shock. He felt a wave of anger, and then a wave of pain: was this the boy he had trained and educated – this wild, ragged, ungrateful wretch, who did not know the difference between what was proper and what was improper, what was civilized and what was barbaric, what was decent and what was shameful – and had the years of training come to nothing? Mr Harrison came out of the shadows and cursed. He brought his hand down on the back of Rusty's neck, propelled him into the drawing room, and pushed him across the room so violently that the boy lost his balance, collided with a table and rolled over on to the ground. Rusty looked up from the floor to find his guardian standing over him, and in the man's right hand was the supple malacca cane, and the cane was twitching.

Mr Harrison's face was twitching too, it was full of fire. His lips were stitched together, sealed up with the ginger moustache, and he looked at the boy with narrowed, unblinking eyes.

'Filth!' he said, almost spitting the words in the boy's face. 'My God, what filth!'

Rusty stared fascinated at the deep yellow nicotine stains on the fingers of his guardian's raised hand. Then the wrist moved suddenly and the cane cut across the boy's face like a knife, stabbing and burning into his cheek.

Rusty cried out and cowered back against the wall; he could feel the blood trickling across his mouth. He looked round desperately for a means of escape, but the man was in front of him, over him, and the wall was behind.

Mr Harrison broke into a torrent of words. 'How can you call yourself an Englishman, how can you come back to this house in such a condition? In what gutter, in what brothel have you been! Have you seen yourself? Do you know what you look like?'

'No,' said Rusty, and for the first time he did not address his guardian as 'sir'. 'I don't care what I look like.'

'You don't . . . well, I'll tell you what you look like! You look like the mongrel that you are!'

'That's a lie!' exclaimed Rusty.

'It's the truth. I've tried to bring you up as an Englishman, as your father would have wished. But, as you won't have it our way, I'm telling you that he was about the only thing English about you. You're no better than the sweeper boy!'

Rusty flared into a temper, showing some spirit for the first time in his life. 'I'm no better than the sweeper boy, but I'm as good as him! I'm as good as you! I'm as good as anyone!' And, instead of cringing to take the cut from the cane, he flung himself at his guardian's legs. The cane swished through the air, grazing the boy's back. Rusty wrapped his arms round his guardian's legs and pulled on them with all his strength.

Mr Harrison went over, falling flat on his back

The suddenness of the fall must have knocked the breath from his body, because for a moment he did not move.

Rusty sprang to his feet. The cut across his face had stung him to madness, to an unreasoning hate, and he did what previously he would only have dreamt of doing. Lifting a vase of the missionary's wife's best sweet peas off the glass cupboard, he flung it at his guardian's face. It hit him on the chest, but the water and flowers flopped out over his face. He tried to get up; but he was speechless.

The look of alarm on Mr Harrison's face gave Rusty greater courage. Before the man could recover his feet and his balance, Rusty gripped him by the collar and pushed him backwards, until they both fell over on to the floor. With one hand still twisting the collar, the boy slapped his guardian's face. Mad with the pain in his own face, Rusty hit the man again and again, wildly and awkwardly, but with the giddy thrill of knowing he could do it: he was a child no longer, he was nearly seventeen, he was a man. He could inflict pain, that was a wonderful discovery; there was a power in his body – a devil or a god – and he gained confidence in his power; and he was a man!

'Stop that, stop it!'

The shout of a hysterical woman brought Rusty to his senses. He still held his guardian by the throat, but he stopped hitting him. Mr Harrison's face was very red.

The missionary's wife stood in the doorway, her face white with fear. She was under the impression that Mr Harrison was being attacked by a servant or some bazaar hooligan. Rusty did not wait until she found her tongue but, with a new-found speed and agility, darted out of the drawing room.

He made his escape from the bedroom window. From the gate he could see the missionary's wife silhouetted against the drawing-room light. He laughed out loud. The woman swivelled round and came forward a few steps.

And Rusty laughed again and began running down the road to the bazaar.

It was late. The smart shops and restaurants were closed. In the bazaar, oil lamps hung outside each doorway; people were asleep on the steps and platforms of shop-fronts, some huddled in blankets, others rolled tight into themselves. The road, which during the day was a busy, noisy crush of people and animals, was quiet and deserted. Only a lean dog still sniffed in the gutter. A woman sang in a room high above the street – a plaintive, tremulous song – and in the far distance a jackal cried to the moon. But the empty, lifeless street was very deceptive; if the roofs could have been removed from but a handful of buildings, it would be seen that life had not really stopped but, beautiful and ugly, persisted through the night.

It was past midnight, though the Clock Tower had no way of saying it. Rusty was in the empty street, and the chaat shop was closed, a sheet of tarpaulin draped across the front. He looked up and down the road, hoping to meet someone he knew; the chaat-wallah, he felt sure, would give him a blanket for the night and a place to sleep; and the next day when Somi came to meet him, he would tell his friend of his predicament, that he had run away from his guardian's house and did not intend returning. But he would have to wait till morning: the chaat shop was shuttered, barred and bolted.

He sat down on the steps; but the stone was cold and his thin cotton pyjamas offered no protection. He folded his arms and huddled up in a corner, but still he shivered. His feet were becoming numb, lifeless.

Rusty had not fully realized the hazards of the situation. He was still mad with anger and rebellion and, though the blood on his cheek had dried, his face was still smarting. He could not think clearly: the present was confusing and unreal and he could not see beyond it; what worried him was the cold and the discomfort and the pain.

The singing stopped in the high window. Rusty looked up and saw a beckoning hand. As no one else in the street showed any signs of life, Rusty got up and walked across the road until he was under the window. The woman pointed to a stairway, and he mounted it, glad of the hospitality he was being offered.

The stairway seemed to go to the stars, but it turned suddenly to lead into the woman's room. The door was slightly ajar, and he knocked and a voice said, 'Come . . .'

The room was filled with perfume and burning incense. A musical instrument lay in one corner. The woman reclined on a bed, her hair scattered about the pillow; she had a round, pretty face, but she was losing her youth, and the fat showed in rolls at her exposed waist. She smiled at the boy, and beckoned again.

'Thank you,' said Rusty, closing the door. 'Can I sleep here?'

'Where else?' said the woman.

'Just for tonight.'

She smiled, and waited. Rusty stood in front of her, his hands behind his back.

'Sit down,' she said, and patted the bedclothes beside her. Reverently, and as respectfully as he could, Rusty sat down.

The woman ran little fair fingers over his body, and drew his head to hers; their lips were very close, almost touching, and their breathing sounded terribly loud to Rusty, but he only said: 'I am hungry.'

A poet, thought the woman, and kissed him full on the lips; but the boy drew away in embarrassment, unsure of himself, liking the woman on the bed and yet afraid of her . . .

'What is wrong?' she asked.

'I'm tired,' he said.

The woman's friendly smile turned to a look of scorn; but she saw that he was only a boy whose eyes were full of unhappiness, and she could not help pitying him.

'You can sleep here,' she said, 'until you have lost your tiredness.'

But he shook his head. 'I will come some other time,' he said, not wishing to hurt the woman's feelings. They were both pitying each other, liking each other, but not enough to make them understand each other.

Rusty left the room. Mechanically, he descended the staircase, and walked up the bazaar road, past the silent sleeping forms, until he reached the Clock Tower. To the right of the Clock Tower was a broad stretch of grassland where, during the day, cattle grazed and children played and young men like Ranbir wrestled and kicked footballs. But now, at night, it was a vast empty space.

But the grass was soft, like the grass in the forest, and Rusty walked the length of the maidan. He found a bench and sat down, warmer for the walk. A light breeze was blowing across the maidan, pleasant and refreshing, playing with his hair. Around him everything was dark and silent and lonely. He had got away from the bazaar, which held the misery of beggars and homeless children and starving dogs, and could now concentrate on his own misery; for there was nothing like loneliness for making Rusty conscious of his unhappy state. Madness and freedom and violence were new to him: loneliness was familiar, something he understood.

Rusty was alone. Until tomorrow, he was alone for the rest of his life.

If tomorrow there was no Somi at the chaat shop, no Ranbir, then what would he do? This question badgered him persistently, making him an unwilling slave to reality. He did not know where his friends lived, he had no money, he could not ask the chaat-wallah for credit on the strength of two visits. Perhaps he should return to the amorous lady in the bazaar; perhaps . . . but no, one thing was certain, he would never return to his guardian . . .

The moon had been hidden by clouds, and presently there was a drizzle. Rusty did not mind the rain, it refreshed him and made the colour run from his body; but, when it began to fall harder, he started shivering again. He felt sick. He got up, rolled his ragged pyjamas up to the thighs and crawled under the bench.

There was a hollow under the bench, and at first Rusty found it quite comfortable. But there was no grass and gradually the earth began to soften: soon he was on his hands and knees in a pool of muddy water, with the slush oozing up through his fingers and toes. Crouching there, wet and cold and muddy, he was overcome by a feeling of helplessness and self-pity: everyone and everything seemed to have turned against him; not only his people but also the bazaar and the chaat shop and even the elements. He admitted to himself that he had been too impulsive in rebelling and running away from home; perhaps there was still time to return and beg Mr Harrison's forgiveness. But could his behaviour be forgiven? Might he not be clapped into irons for attempted murder? Most certainly he would be given another beating: not six strokes this time, but nine.

His only hope was Somi. If not Somi, then Ranbir. If not Ranbir . . . well, it was no use thinking further, there was no one else to think of.

The rain had ceased. Rusty crawled out from under the bench, and stretched his cramped limbs. The moon came out from a cloud, and played with his wet, glistening body, and showed him the vast, naked loneliness of the maidan and his own insignificance. He longed now for the presence of people, be they beggars or women, and he broke into a trot, and the trot became a run, a frightened run, and he did not stop until he reached the Clock Tower.

Chapter Seven

They who sleep last wake first. Hunger and pain lengthen the night, and so the beggars and dogs are the last to see the stars; hunger and pain hasten the awakening, and beggars and dogs are the first to see the sun. Rusty knew hunger and pain, but his weariness was even greater, and he was asleep on the steps of the chaat shop long after the sun had come striding down the road, knocking on nearly every door and window.

Somi bathed at the common water tank. He stood under the tap and slapped his body into life and spluttered with the shock of mountain water.

At the tank were many people: children shrieking with delight – or discomfort – as their ayahs slapped them about roughly and affectionately; the ayahs themselves, strong, healthy hill-women, with heavy bracelets on their ankles; the bhisti – the water-carrier – with his skin bag; and the cook with his pots and pans. The ayahs sat on their haunches, bathing the children, their saris rolled up to the thighs; every time they moved their feet, the bells on their ankles jingled; so that there was a continuous shrieking and jingling and slapping of buttocks. The cook smeared his utensils with ash and washed them, and filled an earthen *chatty* with water; the bhisti hoisted the water bag over his shoulder and left, dripping; a pie-dog lapped at water rolling off the stone platform; and a baleful-looking cow nibbled at wet grass.

It was with these people that Somi spent his mornings, laughing and talking and bathing with them. When he had finished his ablutions, dried his hair in the sun, dressed and tied his turban, he mounted his bicycle and rode out of the compound.

At this advanced hour of the morning Mr Harrison still slept. In the half-empty church, his absence was noted: he seldom missed Sunday morning services; and the missionary's wife was impatiently waiting for the end of the sermon, for she had so much to talk about.

Outside the chaat shop Somi said, 'Hey, Rusty, get up, what has happened? Where is Ranbir? Holi finished yesterday, you know!'

He shook Rusty by the shoulders, shouting into his ear; and the pale boy lying on the stone steps opened his eyes and blinked in the morning sunshine; his eyes roamed about in bewilderment, he could not remember how he came to be lying in the sunshine in the bazaar.

'Hey,' said Somi, 'your guardian will be very angry!'

Rusty sat up with a start. He was wide awake now, sweeping up his scattered thoughts and sorting them out. It was difficult for him to be straightforward; but he forced himself to look Somi straight in the eyes and, very simply and without preamble, say: 'I've run away from home.'

Somi showed no surprise. He did not take his eyes off Rusty's; nor did his expression alter. A half-smile on his lips, he said: 'Good. Now you can come and stay with me.'

Somi took Rusty home on the bicycle. Rusty felt weak in the legs, but his mind was relieved and he no longer felt alone: once again, Somi gave him a feeling of confidence.

'Do you think I can get a job?' asked Rusty.

'Don't worry about that yet, you have only just run away.'

'Do you think I can get a job?' persisted Rusty.

'Why not? But don't worry, you are going to stay with me.'

'I'll stay with you only until I find a job. Any kind of job, there must be something.'

'Of course, don't worry,' said Somi, and pressed harder on the pedals.

They came to a canal; it was noisy with the rush of mountain water, for the snow had begun to melt. The road, which ran parallel to the canal, was flooded in some parts, but Somi steered a steady course. Then the canal turned left and the road kept straight, and presently the sound of water was but a murmur, and the road quiet and shady; there were trees at the roadsides covered in pink and white blossoms, and behind them more trees, thicker and greener; and in amongst the trees were houses.

A boy swung on a creaking wooden gate. He whistled out, and Somi waved back; that was all.

'Who's that?' asked Rusty.

'Son of his parents.'

'What do you mean?'

'His father is rich. So Kishen is somebody. He has money, and it is as powerful as Suri's tongue.'

'Is he Suri's friend or yours?'

'When it suits him, he is our friend. When it suits him, he is Suri's friend.'

'Then he's clever as well as rich,' deduced Rusty.

'The brains are his mother's.'

'And the money his father's?'

'Yes, but there isn't much left now. Kapoor is finished . . . He looks like his father too, his mother is beautiful. Well, here we are!'

Somi rode the bicycle in amongst the trees and along a snaky path that dodged this way and that, and then they reached the house.

It was a small flat house, covered completely by a crimson bougainvillea creeper. The garden was a mass of marigolds, which had sprung up everywhere, even in the cracks at the sides of the veranda steps. No one was at home. Somi's father was in Delhi, and his mother was out for the morning, buying the week's vegetables.

'Have you any brothers?' asked Rusty, as he entered the front room.

'No. But I've got two sisters. But they're married. Come on, let's see if my clothes will fit you.'

Rusty laughed, for he was older and bigger than his friend; but he was thinking in terms of shirts and trousers, the kind of garments he was used to wearing. He sat down on a sofa in the front room, whilst Somi went for the clothes.

The room was cool and spacious, and had very little furniture. But on the walls were many pictures, and in the centre a large one of Guru Nanak, the founder of the Sikh religion: his body bare, the saint sat with his legs crossed and the palms of his hands touching in prayer, and on his face there was a serene expression: the serenity of Nanak's countenance seemed to communicate itself to the room. There was a serenity about Somi too; maybe because of the smile that always hovered near his mouth.

Rusty concluded that Somi's family were middle class people; that is, they were neither rich nor beggars, but managed to live all the same.

Somi came back with the clothes.

'They are mine,' he said, 'so maybe they will be a little small for you. Anyway, the warm weather is coming and it will not matter what you wear – better nothing at all!'

Rusty put on a long white shirt which, to his surprise, hung loose; it had a high collar and broad sleeves.

'It is loose,' he said, 'how can it be yours?'

'It is made loose,' said Somi.

Rusty pulled on a pair of white pyjamas, and they were definitely small for him, ending a few inches above the ankle. The sandals would not buckle; and, when he walked, they behaved like Somi's and slapped against his heels.

'There!' exclaimed Somi in satisfaction. 'Now everything is settled, chaat in your stomach, clean clothes on your body, and in a few days we find a job! Now, is there anything else?'

Rusty knew Somi well enough now to know that it wasn't necessary to thank him for anything; gratitude was taken for granted; in true friendship there are no formalities and no obligations. Rusty did not even ask if Somi had consulted his mother about taking in guests; perhaps she was used to this sort of thing.

'Is there anything else?' repeated Somi.

Rusty yawned. 'Can I go to sleep now, please?'

Chapter Eight

Rusty had never slept well in his guardian's house, because he had never been tired enough; also his imagination would disturb him. And, since running away, he had slept badly, because he had been cold and hungry. But in Somi's house he felt safe and a little happy, and slept; he slept the remainder of the day and through the night.

In the morning Somi tipped Rusty out of bed and dragged him to the water tank. Rusty watched Somi strip and stand under the jet of tap water, and shuddered at the prospect of having to do the same.

Before removing his shirt, Rusty looked around in embarrassment; no one paid much attention to him, though one of the ayahs, the girl with the bangles, gave him a sly smile; he looked away from the women, threw his shirt on a bush and advanced cautiously to the bathing place.

Somi pulled him under the tap. The water was icy cold and Rusty gasped with the shock. As soon as he was wet, he sprang off the platform, much to the amusement of Somi and the ayahs.

There was no towel with which to dry himself; he stood on the grass, shivering with cold, wondering whether he should dash back to the house or shiver in the open until the sun dried him. But the girl with the bangles was beside him holding a towel; her eyes were full of mockery, but her smile was friendly.

At the midday meal, which consisted of curry and curd and chapattis, Rusty met Somi's mother, and liked her.

She was a woman of about thirty-five; she had a few grey hairs at the temples, and her skin – unlike Somi's – was rough and dry. She dressed simply, in a plain white sari. Her life had been difficult. After the partition of the country, when hate made religion its own, Somi's family had to leave their home in the Punjab and trek southwards; they had walked hundreds of miles and the mother had carried Somi, who was then six, on her back. Life in India had to be started again, right from the beginning, for they had lost most of their property: the father found work in Delhi, the sisters were married off, and Somi and his mother settled down in Dehra, where the boy attended school.

The mother said: 'Mister Rusty, you must give Somi a few lessons in spelling and arithmetic. Always, he comes last in class.'

'Oh, that's good!' exclaimed Somi. 'We'll have fun, Rusty!' Then he thumped the table. 'I have an idea! I know, I think I have a job for you! Remember Kishen, the boy we passed yesterday? Well, his father wants someone to give him private lessons in English.'

'Teach Kishen?'

'Yes, it will be easy. I'll go and see Kapoor and tell him I've found a professor of English or something like that, and then you can come and see him. Brother, it is a first-class idea, you are going to be a teacher!'

Rusty felt very dubious about the proposal; he was not sure he could teach English or anything else to the wilful son of a rich man; but he was not in a position to pick and choose. Somi mounted his bicycle and rode off to see Kapoor to secure for Rusty the post of Professor of English. When he returned he seemed pleased with himself, and Rusty's heart sank with the knowledge that he had got a job.

'You are to come and see him this evening,' announced Somi, 'he will tell you all about it. They want a teacher for Kishen, especially if they don't have to pay.'

'What kind of a job without pay?' complained Rusty.

'No pay,' said Somi, 'but everything else. Food – and no cooking is better than Punjabi cooking; water –'

'I should hope so,' said Rusty.

'And a room, sir!'

'Oh, even a room,' said Rusty ungratefully, 'that will be nice.'

'Anyway,' said Somi, 'come and see him, you don't have to accept.'

The house the Kapoors lived in was very near the canal; it was a squat, comfortable-looking bungalow, surrounded by uncut hedges, and shaded by banana and papaya trees. It was late evening when Somi and Rusty arrived, and the moon was up, and the shaggy branches of the banana trees shook their heavy shadows out over the gravel path.

In an open space in front of the house a log fire was burning; the Kapoors appeared to be giving a party. Somi and Rusty joined the people who were grouped round the fire, and Rusty wondered if he had been invited to the party. The fire lent a friendly warmth to the chilly night, and the flames leapt up, casting the glow of roses on people's faces.

Somi pointed out different people: various shopkeepers, one or two Big Men, the sickly-looking Suri (who was never absent from a social occasion such as this) and a few total strangers who had invited themselves to the party just for the fun of the thing and a free meal. Kishen, the Kapoors' son, was not present; he hated parties, preferring the company of certain wild friends in the bazaar.

Kapoor was once a Big Man himself, and everyone knew this; but he had fallen from the heights; and, until he gave up the bottle, was not likely to reach them again. Everyone felt sorry for his wife, including herself.

Presently Kapoor tottered out of the front door arm-in-arm with a glass and a bottle of whisky. He wore a green dressing gown and a week's beard; his hair, or what was left of it, stood up on end; and he dribbled slightly. An awkward silence fell on the company; but Kapoor, who was a friendly, gentle sort of drunkard, looked round benevolently, and said: 'Everybody here? Fine, fine, they are all here, all of them . . . Throw some more wood on the fire!'

The fire was doing very well indeed, but not well enough for Kapoor; every now and then he would throw a log on the flames until it was feared the blaze would reach the house. Meena, Kapoor's wife, did not look flustered, only irritated; she was a capable person, still young, a charming hostess; and in her red sari and white silk jacket, her hair plaited and scented with jasmine, she looked beautiful. Rusty gazed admiringly at her; he wanted to compliment her, to say, 'Mrs Kapoor, you are beautiful'; but he had no need to tell her, she was fully conscious of the fact.

Meena made her way over to one of the Big Men, and whispered something in his ear, and then she went to a Little Shopkeeper and whispered something in his ear, and then both the Big Man and the Little Shopkeeper advanced stealthily towards the spot where Kapoor was holding forth, and made a gentle attempt to convey him indoors.

But Kapoor was having none of it. He pushed the men aside and roared: 'Keep the fire burning! Keep it burning, don't let it go out, throw some more wood on it!'

And before he could be restrained, he had thrown a pot of the most delicious sweetmeats on to the flames.

To Rusty this was sacrilege. 'Oh, Kapoor . . .' he cried, but there was some confusion in the rear, and his words were drowned in a series of explosions.

Suri and one or two others had begun letting off fireworks: fountains, rockets, and explosives. The fountains gushed forth in green and red and silver lights, and the rockets struck through the night with crimson tails; but it was the explosives that caused the confusion.

The guests did not know whether to press forward into the fire, or retreat amongst the fireworks; neither prospect was pleasing, and the women began to show signs of hysterics. Then Suri burnt his finger and began screaming, and this was all the women had been waiting for; headed by Suri's mother, they rushed the boy and smothered him with attention; whilst the men, who were in a minority, looked on sheepishly and wished the accident had been of a more serious nature.

Something rough brushed against Rusty's cheek.

It was Kapoor's beard. Somi had brought his host to Rusty, and the bemused man put his face close to Rusty's and placed his hands on the boy's shoulders in order to steady himself. Kapoor nodded his head, his eyes red and watery.

'Rusty . . . so you are Mister Rusty . . . I hear you are going to be my schoolteacher.'

'Your son's, sir,' said Rusty, 'but that is for you to decide.'

'Do not call me "sir",' he said, wagging his finger in Rusty's face, 'call me by my name. So you are going to England, eh?'

'No, I'm going to be your schoolteacher.' Rusty had to put his arm round Kapoor's waist to avoid being dragged to the ground; Kapoor leant heavily on the boy's shoulders.

'Good, good. Tell me after you have gone, I want to give you some addresses of people I know. You must go to

Monte Carlo, you've seen nothing until you've seen Monte Carlo, it's the only place with a future . . . Who built Monte Carlo, do you know?'

It was impossible for Rusty to make any sense of the conversation or discuss his appointment as Professor of English to Kishen Kapoor. Kapoor began to slip from his arms, and the boy took the opportunity of changing his own position for a more comfortable one, before levering his host up again. The amused smiles of the company rested on this little scene.

Rusty said: 'No, Kapoor, who built Monte Carlo?'

'I did. I built Monte Carlo!'

'Oh yes, of course.'

'Yes, I built this house, I'm a genius, there's no doubt of it! I have a high opinion of my own opinion, what is yours?'

'Oh, I don't know, but I'm sure you're right.'

'Of course I am. But speak up, don't be afraid to say what you think. Stand up for your rights, even if you're wrong! Throw some more wood on the fire, keep it burning.'

Kapoor leapt from Rusty's arms and stumbled towards the fire. The boy cried a warning and, catching hold of the end of the green dressing gown, dragged his host back to safety. Meena ran to them and, without so much as a glance at Rusty, took her husband by the arm and propelled him indoors.

Rusty stared after Meena Kapoor, and continued to stare even when she had disappeared. The guests chattered pleasantly, pretending nothing had happened, keeping the gossip for the next morning; but the children giggled amongst themselves, and the devil Suri shouted: 'Throw some more wood on the fire, keep it burning!'

Somi returned to his friend's side. 'What did Kapoor have to say?'

'He said he built Monte Carlo.'

Somi slapped his forehead. '*Toba!* Now we'll have to come again tomorrow evening. And then, if he's drunk, we'll have to discuss with his wife, she's the only one with any sense.'

They walked away from the party, out of the circle of firelight, into the shadows of the banana trees. The voices of the guests became a distant murmur: Suri's high-pitched shout came to them on the clear, still air.

Somi said: 'We must go to the chaat shop tomorrow morning, Ranbir is asking for you.'

Rusty had almost forgotten Ranbir; he felt ashamed for not having asked about him before this. Ranbir was an important person, he had changed the course of Rusty's life with nothing but a little colour, red and green, and the touch of his hand.

Chapter Nine

Against his parents' wishes, Kishen Kapoor spent most of his time in the bazaar; he loved it because it was forbidden, because it was unhealthy, dangerous and full of germs to carry home.

Ranbir loved the bazaar because he was born in it; he had known few other places. Since the age of ten he had looked after his uncle's buffaloes, grazing them on the maidan and taking them down to the river to wallow in mud and water; and in the evening he took them home, riding on the back of the strongest and fastest animal. When he grew older, he was allowed to help in his father's cloth shop, but he was always glad to get back to the buffaloes.

Kishen did not like animals, particularly cows and buffaloes. His greatest enemy was Maharani, the Queen of the Bazaar, who, like Kishen, was spoilt and pampered and fond of having her own way. Unlike other cows, she did not feed at dustbins and rubbish heaps, but lived on the benevolence of the bazaar people.

But Kishen had no time for religion; to him a cow was just a cow, nothing sacred; and he saw no reason why he should get off the pavement in order to make way for one, or offer no protest when it stole from under his nose. One day, he tied an empty tin to Maharani's tail and looked on in great enjoyment as the cow pranced madly and dangerously about the road, the tin clattering behind her. Lacking in dignity, Kishen found some pleasure in observing others lose theirs. But a few days later Kishen received Maharani's nose in his pants, and had to pick himself up from the gutter.

Kishen and Ranbir ate mostly at the chaat shop; if they had no money they went to work in Ranbir's uncle's sugar cane fields and earned a rupee for the day; but Kishen did not like work, and Ranbir had enough of his own to do, so there was never much money for chaat; which meant living on their wits – or, rather, Kishen's wits, for it was his duty to pocket any spare money that might be lying about in his father's house – and sometimes helping themselves at the fruit and vegetable stalls when no one was looking.

Ranbir wrestled. That was why he was so good at riding buffaloes. He was the best wrestler in the bazaar; not very clever, but powerful; he was like a great tree, and no amount of shaking could move him from whatever spot he chose to plant his big feet. But he was gentle by nature. The women always gave him their babies to look after when they were busy, and he would cradle the babies in his open hands, and sing to them, and be happy for hours.

Ranbir had a certain innocence which was not likely to leave him. He had seen and experienced life to the full, and life had bruised and scarred him but it had not crippled him. One night he strayed unwittingly into the intoxicating arms of a local temple dancing girl; but he acted with instinct, his pleasure was unpremeditated, and the adventure was soon forgotten – by Ranbir. But Suri, the scourge of the bazaar, uncovered a few facts and threatened to inform Ranbir's family of the incident; and so Ranbir found himself in the power of the cunning Suri, and was forced to please him from time to time; though, at times such as the Holi festival, that power was scorned.

On the morning after the Kapoors' party, Ranbir, Somi and Rusty were seated in the chaat shop, discussing Rusty's situation. Ranbir looked miserable; his hair fell sadly over his forehead, and he would not look at Rusty.

'I have got you into trouble,' he apologized gruffly, 'I am too ashamed.'

Rusty laughed, licking sauce from his fingers and crumpling up his empty leaf bowl.

'Silly fellow,' he said, 'for what are you sorry? For making me happy? For taking me away from my guardian? Well, I am not sorry, you can be sure of that.'

'You are not angry?' asked Ranbir in wonder.

'No, but you will make me angry in this way.'

Ranbir's face lit up, and he slapped Somi and Rusty on their backs with such sudden enthusiasm that Somi dropped his bowl of allu chole.

'Come on, misters,' he said, 'I am going to make you sick with gol guppas so that you will not be able to eat any more until I return from Mussoorie!'

'Mussoorie?' Somi looked puzzled. 'You are going to Mussoorie?'

'To school!'

'That's right,' said a voice from the door, a voice hidden in smoke.

'Now we've had it . . .' Somi said. 'It's that monkey-millionaire Kishen come to make a nuisance of himself.' Then, louder: 'Come over here, Kishen, come and join us for gol gappas!'

Kishen appeared from the mist of vapour, walking with an affected swagger, his hands in his pockets; he was the only one present wearing pants instead of pyjamas.

'Hey!' exclaimed Somi. 'Who has given you a black eye?'

Kishen did not answer immediately, but sat down opposite Rusty. His shirt hung over his pants, and his pants hung over his knees; he had bushy eyebrows and hair, and a drooping, disagreeable mouth; the sulky expression on his face had become a permanent one, not a mood of the moment. Kishen's swagger, money, unattractive face and qualities made him – for Rusty, anyway – curiously attractive . . .

He prodded his nose with his forefinger, as he always did when a trifle excited. 'Those damn wrestlers, they piled on to me.'

'Why?' said Ranbir, sitting up instantly.

'I was making a badminton court on the maidan, and these fellows came along and said they had reserved the place for a wrestling ground.'

'So then?'

Kishen's affected American twang became more pronounced. 'I told them to go to hell!'

Ranbir laughed. 'So they all started wrestling you?'

'Yeah, but I didn't know they would hit me too. I bet

if you fellows were there, they wouldn't have tried anything. Isn't that so, Ranbir?'

Ranbir smiled; he knew it was so, but did not care to speak of his physical prowess. Kishen took notice of the newcomer.

'Are you Mister Rusty?' he asked.

'Yes, I am,' said the boy. 'Are you Mister Kishen?'

'I am Mister Kishen. You know how to box, Rusty?'

'Well,' said the boy, unwilling to become involved in a local feud, 'I've never boxed wrestlers.'

Somi changed the subject. 'Rusty's coming to see your father this evening. You must try and persuade your pop to give him the job of teaching you English.'

Kishen prodded his nose, and gave Rusty a sly wink.

'Yes, Daddy told me about you, he says you are a professor. You can be my teacher on the condition that we don't work too hard, and you support me when I tell them lies, and that you tell them I am working hard. Sure, you can be my teacher, sure . . . better you than a real one.'

'I'll try to please everyone,' said Rusty.

'You're a clever person if you can. But I think you are clever.'

'Yes,' agreed Rusty, and was inwardly amazed at the way he spoke.

*

As Rusty had now met Kishen, Somi suggested that the two should go to the Kapoors' house together; so that evening, Rusty met Kishen in the bazaar and walked home with him.

There was a crowd in front of the bazaar's only cinema, and it was getting restive and demonstrative. One had to fight to get into this particular cinema, as there was no organized queuing or booking.

'Is anything wrong?' asked Rusty.

'Oh, no,' said Kishen, 'it is just Laurel and Hardy today, they are very popular. Whenever a popular film is shown, there is usually a riot. But I know of a way in through the roof; I'll show you some time.'

'Sounds crazy.'

'Yeah, the roof leaks, so people usually bring their umbrellas. Also their food, because when the projector breaks down or the electricity fails, we have to wait a long time. Sometimes, when it is a long wait, the chaat-wallah comes in and does some business.'

'Sounds crazy,' repeated Rusty.

'You'll get used to it. Have a chewing gum.'

Kishen's jaws had been working incessantly on a lump of gum that had been increasing in size over the last three days; he started on a fresh stick every hour or so, without throwing away the old ones. Rusty was used to seeing Indians chew paan, the betel leaf preparation which stained the mouth with red juices, but Kishen wasn't like any of the Indians Rusty had met so far. He accepted a stick of gum, and the pair walked home in silent concentration, their jaws moving rhythmically, and Kishen's tongue making sudden sucking sounds.

As they entered the front room, Meena Kapoor pounced on Kishen.

'Ah! So you have decided to come home at last! And what do you mean by asking Daddy for money without letting me know? What have you done with it, Kishen bhaiya? Where is it?'

Kishen sauntered across the room and deposited himself on the couch. 'I've spent it.'

Meena's hands went to her hips. 'What do you mean, you've spent it!'

'I mean I've eaten it.'

He got two resounding slaps across his face, and his flesh went white where his mother's fingers left their mark. Rusty backed towards the door; it was embarrassing to be present at this intimate family scene.

'Don't go, Rusty,' shouted Kishen, 'or she won't stop slapping me!'

Kapoor, still wearing his green dressing gown and beard, came in from the adjoining room, and his wife turned on him.

'Why do you give the child so much money?' she demanded. 'You know he spends it on nothing but bazaar food and makes himself sick.'

Rusty seized at the opportunity of pleasing the whole family; of saving Kapoor's skin, pacifying his wife, and gaining the affection and regard of Kishen.

'It is all my fault,' he said, 'I took Kishen to the chaat shop. I'm very sorry.'

Meena Kapoor became quiet and her eyes softened; but Rusty resented her kindly expression because he knew it was prompted by pity – pity for him – and a satisfied pride. Meena was proud because she thought her son had shared his money with one who apparently hadn't any.

'I did not see you come in,' she said.

'I only wanted to explain about the money.'

'Come in, don't be shy.'

Meena's smile was full of kindness, but Rusty was not looking for kindness; for no apparent reason, he felt lonely; he missed Somi, felt lost without him, helpless and clumsy.

'There is another thing,' he said, remembering the post of Professor in English.

'But come in, Mister Rusty . . .'

It was the first time she had used his name, and the gesture immediately placed them on equal terms. She was a graceful woman, much younger than Kapoor; her features had a clear, classic beauty, and her voice was gentle but firm. Her hair was tied in a neat bun and laced with a string of jasmine flowers.

'Come in . . .'

'About teaching Kishen,' mumbled Rusty.

'Come and play carom,' said Kishen from the couch. 'We are none of us any good. Come and sit down, pardner.'

'He fancies himself as an American,' said Meena. 'If ever you see him in the cinema, drag him out.'

The carom board was brought in from the next room, and it was arranged that Rusty partner Kapoor. They began play, but the game didn't progress very fast because Kapoor kept leaving the table in order to disappear behind a screen, from the direction of which came a tinkle of bottles and glasses. Rusty was afraid of Kapoor getting drunk before he could be approached about the job of teaching Kishen.

'My wife,' said Kapoor in a loud whisper to Rusty, 'does not let me drink in public any more, so I have to do it in a cupboard.'

He looked sad; there were tear stains on his cheeks; the tears were caused not by Meena's scolding, which he ignored, but by his own self-pity; he often cried for himself, usually in his sleep.

Whenever Rusty pocketed one of the carom men, Kapoor exclaimed: 'Ah, nice shot, nice shot!' as though it were a cricket match they were playing. 'But hit it slowly, slowly . . .' And when it was his turn, he gave the striker a feeble push, moving it a bare inch from his finger.

'Play properly,' murmured Meena, who was intent on winning the game; but Kapoor would be up from his seat again, and the company would sit back and wait for the tune of clinking glass.

It was a very irritating game. Kapoor insisted on showing Rusty how to strike the men; and whenever Rusty made a mistake, Meena said 'thank you' in an amused and conceited manner that angered the boy. When she and Kishen had cleared the board of whites, Kapoor and Rusty were left with eight blacks.

'Thank you,' said Meena sweetly.

'We are too good for you,' scoffed Kishen, busily arranging the board for another game.

Kapoor took sudden interest in the proceedings: 'Who won, I say, who won?'

Much to Rusty's disgust, they began another game, and with the same partners; but they had just started when Kapoor flopped forward and knocked the carom board off the table. He had fallen asleep. Rusty took him by the shoulders, eased him back into the chair. Kapoor's breathing was heavy; saliva had collected at the sides of his mouth, and he snorted a little.

Rusty thought it was time he left. Rising from the table, he said, 'I will have to ask another time about the job . . .'

'Hasn't he told you as yet?' said Meena.

'What?'

'That you can have the job.'

'Can I!' exclaimed Rusty.

Meena gave a little laugh. 'But of course! Certainly there is no one else who would take it on, Kishen is not easy to teach. There is no fixed pay, but we will give you anything you need. You are not our servant. You will be doing us a favour by giving Kishen some of your knowledge and conversation and company, and in return we will be giving you our hospitality. You will have a room of your own, and your food you will have with us. What do you think?'

'Oh, it is wonderful!' said Rusty.

And it was wonderful, and he felt gay and lightheaded, and all the troubles in the world scurried away; he even felt successful: he had a profession. And Meena Kapoor was smiling at him, and looking more beautiful than she really was, and Kishen was saying:

'Tomorrow you must stay till twelve o'clock, all right, even if Daddy goes to sleep. Promise me?'

Rusty promised.

An unaffected enthusiasm was bubbling up in Kishen; it was quite different to the sulkiness of his usual manner. Rusty had liked him in spite of the younger boy's unattractive qualities, and now liked him more; for Kishen had taken Rusty into his home and confidence without knowing him very well and without asking any questions. Kishen was a scoundrel, a monkey – crude and well-spoilt – but, for him to have taken a liking to Rusty (and Rusty held himself in high esteem), he must have some virtues . . . or so Rusty reasoned.

His mind, while he walked back to Somi's house, dwelt on his relationship with Kishen; but his tongue, when he loosened it in Somi's presence, dwelt on Meena Kapoor. And when he lay down to sleep, he saw her in his mind's eye, and for the first time took conscious note of her beauty, of her warmth and softness; and made up his mind that he would fall in love with her.

Chapter Ten

Mr Harrison was back to normal in a few days, and telling everyone of Rusty's barbaric behaviour.

'If he wants to live like an animal, he can. He left my house of his own free will, and I feel no responsibility for him. It's his own fault if he starves to death.'

The missionary's wife said: 'But I do hope you will forgive him if he returns.'

'I will, madam. I have to. I'm his legal guardian. And I hope he doesn't return.'

'Oh, Mr Harrison, he's only a boy . . .'

'That's what you think.'

'I'm sure he'll come back.'

Mr Harrison shrugged indifferently.

Rusty's thoughts were far from his guardian. He was listening to Meena Kapoor tell him about his room, and he gazed into her eyes all the time she talked.

'It is a very nice room,' she said, 'but of course there is no water or electricity or lavatory.'

Rusty was bathing in the brown pools of her eyes.

She said: 'You will have to collect your water at the big tank, and for the rest, you will have to do it in the jungle . . .'

Rusty thought he saw his own gaze reflected in her eyes.

'Yes?' he said.

'You can give Kishen his lessons in the morning until twelve o'clock. Then no more, then you have your food.'

'Then?'

He watched the movement of her lips.

'Then nothing, you do what you like, go out with Kishen or Somi or any of your friends.'

'Where do I teach Kishen?'

'On the roof, of course.'

Rusty retrieved his gaze, and scratched his head. The roof seemed a strange place for setting up school.

'Why the roof?'

'Because your room is on the roof.'

*

Meena led the boy round the house until they came to a flight of steps, unsheltered, that went up to the roof. They had to hop over a narrow drain before climbing the steps.

'This drain,' warned Meena, 'is very easy to cross. But when you are coming downstairs be sure not to take too big a step because then you might bump the wall on the other side or fall over the stove which is usually there . . .'

'I'll be careful,' said Rusty.

They began climbing, Meena in the lead. Rusty watched Meena's long, slender feet. The slippers she wore consisted only of two straps that passed between her toes, and the backs of the slippers slapped against her heels like Somi's, only the music – like the feet – was different . . .

'Another thing about these steps,' continued Meena, 'there are twenty-two of them. No, don't count, I have already done so . . . But remember, if you are coming home in the dark, be sure you take only twenty-two steps, because if you don't, then' – and she snapped her fingers in the air – 'you will be finished! After twenty-two steps you turn right and you find the door, here it is. If you do not turn right and you take *twenty-three* steps, you will go over the edge of the roof!'

They both laughed, and suddenly Meena took Rusty's hand and led him into the room.

It was a small room, but this did not matter much as there was very little in it: only a string bed, a table, a shelf and a few nails in the wall. In comparison to Rusty's room in his guardian's house, it wasn't even a room: it was four walls, a door and a window.

The door looked out on the roof, and Meena pointed through it, at the big round water tank.

'That is where you bathe and get your water,' she said.

'I know, I went with Somi.'

There was a big mango tree behind the tank, and Kishen was sitting in its branches, watching them. Surrounding the house were a number of litchee trees, and in the summer they and the mango would bear fruit.

Meena and Rusty stood by the window in silence, hand in hand. Rusty was prepared to stand there, holding hands forever. Meena felt a sisterly affection for him; but he was stumbling into love.

From the window they could see many things. In the distance, towering over the other trees, was the Flame of the Forest, its flowers glowing red-hot against the blue of the sky. Through the window came a shoot of pink bougainvillea creeper; and Rusty knew he would never cut it; and so he knew he would never be able to shut the window.

Meena said, 'If you do not like it, we will find another . . .'

Rusty squeezed her hand, and smiled into her eyes, and said: 'But I like it. This is the room I want to live in. And do you know why, Meena? Because it isn't a real room, that's why!'

The afternoon was warm, and Rusty sat beneath the big banyan tree that grew behind the house, a tree that was almost a house in itself; its spreading branches drooped to the ground and took new root, forming a maze of pillared passages. The tree sheltered scores of birds and squirrels.

A squirrel stood in front of Rusty. It looked at him from between its legs, its tail in the air, back arched gracefully and nose quivering excitedly.

'Hullo,' said Rusty.

The squirrel brushed its nose with its forepaw, winked at the boy, hopped over his leg, and ran up a pillar of the banyan tree.

Rusty leant back against the broad trunk of the banyan, and listened to the lazy drone of the bees, the squeaking of the squirrels and the incessant bird talk.

He thought of Meena and of Kishen, and felt miserably happy; and then he remembered Somi and the chaat shop.

The chaat-wallah, that god of the tikkees, handed Rusty a leaf bowl, and prepared allu chole: first sliced potatoes, then peas, then red and gold chilli powders, then a sprinkling of juices, then he shook it all up and down in the leaf bowl and, in a simplicity, the allu chole was ready.

Somi removed his slippers, crossed his legs, and looked a question.

'It's fine,' said Rusty.

'You are sure?'

There was concern in Somi's voice, and his eyes seemed to hesitate a little before smiling with the mouth.

'It's fine,' said Rusty. 'I'll soon get used to the room.'

There was a silence. Rusty concentrated on the allu chole, feeling guilty and ungrateful.

'Ranbir has gone,' said Somi.

'Oh, he didn't even say goodbye!'

'He has not gone forever. And anyway, what would be the use of saying goodbye . . .'

He sounded depressed. He finished his allu chole and said: 'Rusty, best favourite friend, if you don't want this job I'll find you another.'

'But I like it, Somi, I want it, really I do. You are trying to do too much for me. Mrs Kapoor is wonderful, and Kapoor is good fun, and Kishen is not so bad, you know . . . Come on to the house and see the room. It's the kind of room in which you write poetry or create music.'

They walked home in the evening. The evening was full of sounds. Rusty noticed the sounds, because he was happy, and a happy person notices things.

Carriages passed them on the road, creaking and rattling, wheels squeaking, hoofs resounding on the ground; and the whip-cracks above the horse's ear, and the driver shouts, and round go the wheels, squeaking and creaking, and the hoofs go *clippety-clippety, clip-clop-clop* . . .

A bicycle came swishing through the puddles, the wheels purring and humming smoothly, the bell tinkling . . . In the bushes there was the chatter of sparrows and seven-sisters, but Rusty could not see them no matter how hard he looked.

And there were footsteps . . .

Their own footsteps, quiet and thoughtful; and ahead of them an old man, with a dhoti round his legs and a black umbrella in his hand, walking at a clockwork pace. At each alternate step he tapped with his umbrella on the pavement; he wore noisy shoes, and his footsteps echoed off the pavement to the beat of the umbrella. Rusty and Somi quickened their own steps, passed him by, and let the endless tapping die on the wind.

They sat on the roof for an hour, watching the sun set, and Somi sang.

Somi had a beautiful voice, clear and mellow, matching the serenity of his face. And when he sang, his eyes wandered into the night, and he was lost to the world and to Rusty; for when he sang of the stars, he was of the stars, and when he sang of a river, he was a river. He communicated his mood to Rusty, as he could not have done in plain language; and, when the song ended, the silence returned and all the world fell asleep.

Chapter Eleven

Rusty watched the dawn blossom into light.

At first everything was dark, then gradually objects began to take shape – the desk and chair, the walls of the room – and the darkness lifted like the raising of a veil, and over the treetops the sky was streaked with crimson. It was like this for some time, while everything became clearer and more distinguishable; and then, when nature was ready, the sun reached up over the trees and hills, and sent one tentative beam of warm light through the window. Along the wall crept the sun, across to the bed, and up the boy's bare legs, until it was caressing his entire body and whispering to him to get up, get up, it is time to get up . . .

Rusty blinked. He sat up and rubbed his eyes and looked around. It was his first morning in the room, and perched on the window sill was a small brown and yellow bird, a maina, looking at him with its head cocked to one side. The maina was a common sight, but this one was unusual: it was bald: all the feathers had been knocked off its head in a series of fights.

Rusty wondered if he should get up and bathe, or wait for someone to arrive. But he didn't wait long. Something bumped him from under the bed.

He stiffened with apprehension. Something was moving beneath him, the mattress rose gently and fell. Could it be a jackal or a wolf that had stolen in through the open door during the night? Rusty trembled, but did not move . . . It might be something even more dangerous, the house was close to the jungle . . . or it might be a thief . . . but what was there to steal?

Unable to bear the suspense, Rusty brought his fists down on the uneven lump in the quilt, and Kishen sprang out with a cry of pain and astonishment.

He sat on his bottom and cursed Rusty.

'Sorry,' said Rusty, 'but you frightened me.'

'I'm glad, because you hurt me, mister.'

'Your fault. What's the time?'

'Time to get up. I've brought you some milk, and you can have mine too. I hate it, it spoils the flavour of my chewing gum.'

Kishen accompanied Rusty to the water tank, where they met Somi. After they had bathed and filled their *sohrais* with drinking water, they went back to the room for the first lesson.

Kishen and Rusty sat cross-legged on the bed, facing each other. Rusty fingered his chin, and Kishen played with his toes.

'What do you want to learn today?' asked Rusty.

'How should I know? That's your problem, pardner.'

'As it's the first day, you can make a choice.'

'Let's play noughts and crosses.'

'Be serious. Tell me, bhaiya, what books have you read?'

Kishen turned his eyes up to the ceiling. 'I've read so many I can't remember the names.'

'Well, you can tell me what they were about.'

Kishen looked disconcerted. 'Oh, sure . . . sure . . . let me see now . . . what about the one in which everyone went down a rabbit hole?'

'What about it?'

'Called *Treasure Island*.'

'Hell!' said Rusty.

'Which ones have you read?' asked Kishen, warming to the discussion.

'*Treasure Island* and the one about the rabbit hole, and you haven't read either. What do you want to be when you grow up, Kishen? A businessman, an officer, an engineer?'

'Don't want to be anything. What about you?'

'You're not supposed to be asking me. But if you want to know, I'm going to be a writer. I'll write books. You'll read them.'

'You'll be a great writer, Rusty, you'll be great . . .'

'Maybe, who knows.'

'I know,' said Kishen, quite sincerely, 'you'll be a terrific writer. You'll be famous. You'll be a king.'

'Shut up . . .'

The Kapoors liked Rusty. They didn't admire him, but they liked him. Kishen liked him for his company, Kapoor liked him for his flattering conversation, and Meena liked him because – well, because he liked her . . .

The Kapoors were glad to have him in their house.

Meena had been betrothed to Kapoor since childhood, before they knew each other, and despite the fact that there was a difference of nearly twenty years between their ages. Kapoor was a promising young man, intelligent and beginning to make money; and Meena, at thirteen, possessed the freshness and promise of spring. After they were married, they fell in love.

They toured Europe, and Kapoor returned a connoisseur of wine. Kishen was born, looking just like his father.

Kapoor never stopped loving his wife, but his passion for her was never so great as when the warmth of old wine filled him with poetry. Meena had a noble nose and forehead ('Aristocratic,' said Kapoor; 'she has blue blood') and long raven-black hair ('Like seaweed,' said Kapoor, dizzy with possessive glory). She was tall, strong, perfectly formed, and she had grace and charm and a quick wit.

Kapoor lived in his beard and green dressing gown, something of an outcast. The self-made man likes to boast of humble origins and initial poverty, and his rise from rags can be turned to effective publicity; the man who has lost much recalls past exploits and the good name of his family, and the failure at least publicizes these things. But Kapoor had gone full cycle: he could no longer harp on the rise from rags, because he was fast becoming ragged; and he had no background except the one which he himself created and destroyed; he had nothing but a dwindling bank balance, a wife and a son. And the wife was his best asset.

But on the evening of Rusty's second day in the room, no one would have guessed at the family's plight. Rusty sat with them in the front room, and Kapoor extolled the virtues of chewing gum, much to Kishen's delight and Meena's disgust.

'Chewing gum,' declared Kapoor, waving a finger in the air, 'is the secret of youth. Have you observed the Americans, how young they look, and the English, how haggard? It has nothing to do with responsibilities, it is chewing gum. By chewing, you exercise your jaws and the muscles of your face. This improves your complexion and strengthens the tissues of your skin.'

'You're very clever, Daddy,' said Kishen.

'I'm a genius,' said Kapoor, 'I'm a genius.'

'The fool!' whispered Meena, so that only Rusty could hear.

Rusty said, 'I have an idea, let's form a club.'

'Good idea!' exclaimed Kishen. 'What do we call it?'

'Before we call it anything, we must decide what sort of club it should be. We must have rules, we must have a president, a secretary . . .'

'All right, all right,' interrupted Kishen, who was sprawling on the floor, 'you can be all those things if you like. But what I say is, the most important thing in a club is the name. Without a good name, what's the use of a club?'

'The Fools' Club,' suggested Meena.

'Inappropriate,' said Kapoor, 'inappropriate . . .'

'Everyone shut up,' ordered Kishen, prodding at his nose, 'I'm trying to think.'

They all shut up and tried to think.

This thinking was a very complicated process, and it soon became obvious that no one had been thinking of the club; for Rusty was looking at Meena thinking, and Meena was wondering if Kishen knew how to think, and Kishen was really thinking about the benefits of chewing gum, and Kapoor was smelling the whisky bottles behind the screen and thinking of them.

At last Kapoor observed: 'My wife is a devil, a beautiful, beautiful devil!'

This seemed an interesting line of conversation, and Rusty was about to follow it up with a compliment of his own, when Kishen burst out brilliantly: 'I know! The Devil's Club? How's that?'

'Ah, ha!' exclaimed Kapoor. 'The Devil's Club, we've got it! I'm a genius.'

They got down to the business of planning the club's activities. Kishen proposed carom and Meena seconded, and Rusty looked dismayed. Kapoor proposed literary and political discussions and Rusty, just to spite the others, seconded the proposal. Then they elected officers of the club. Meena was given the title of Our Lady and Patroness, Kapoor was elected President, Rusty the Secretary, and Kishen the Chief Whip. Somi, Ranbir and Suri, though absent, were accepted as Honorary Members.

'Carom and discussions are not enough,' complained Kishen, 'we must have adventures.'

'What kind?' asked Rusty. 'Climb mountains or something?'

'A picnic,' proposed Meena.

'A picnic!' seconded Kishen. 'And Somi and the others can come too.'

'Let's drink to it,' said Kapoor, rising from his chair, 'let's celebrate.'

'Good idea,' said Kishen, foiling his father's plan of action, 'we'll go to the chaat shop!'

As far as Meena was concerned, the chaat shop was the lesser of the two evils, so Kapoor was bundled into the old car and taken to the bazaar.

'To the chaat shop!' he cried, falling across the steering wheel. 'We will bring it home!'

The chaat shop was so tightly crowded that people were breathing each other's breath.

The chaat-wallah was very pleased with Rusty for bringing in so many new customers – a whole family – and beamed on the party, rubbing his hands and greasing the frying pan with enthusiasm.

'Everything!' ordered Kapoor. 'We will have something of everything.'

So the chaat-wallah patted his cakes into shape and flipped them into the sizzling grease; and fashioned his gol guppas over the fire, filling them with the juice of the devil.

Meena sat curled up on a chair, facing Rusty. The boy stared at her: she looked quaint, sitting in this unfamiliar posture. Her eyes encountered Rusty's stare, mocking it. In hot confusion, Rusty moved his eyes upward, up the wall, on to the ceiling, until they could go no further.

'What are you looking at?' asked Kishen.

Rusty brought his eyes to the ground, and pretended not to have heard. He turned to Kapoor and said, 'What about politics?'

The chaat-wallah handed out four big banana leaves.

But Kapoor wouldn't eat. Instead, he cried: 'Take the chaat shop to the house. Put it in the car, we must have it! We must have it, we must have it!'

The chaat-wallah, who was used to displays of drunkenness in one form or another, humoured Kapoor. 'It is all yours, Lallaji, but take me with you too, or who will run the shop?'

'We will!' shouted Kishen, infected by his father's enthusiasm. 'Buy it, Daddy. Mummy can make the tikkees and I'll sell them and Rusty can do the accounts!'

Kapoor threw his banana leaf of the floor and wrapped his arms round Kishen. 'Yes, we will run it! Take it to the house!' And, making a lunge at a bowl of chaat, fell to his knees.

Rusty helped Kapoor get up, then looked to Meena for guidance. She said nothing, but gave him a nod, and the boy found he understood the nod.

He said, 'It's a wonderful idea, Kapoor, just put me in charge of everything. You and Meena go home and get a spare room ready for the supplies, and Kishen and I will make all the arrangements with the chaat-wallah.'

Kapoor clung to Rusty, the spittle dribbling down his cheeks. 'Good boy, good boy . . . we will make lots of money together, you and I . . .' He turned to his wife and waved his arm grandiloquently: 'We will be rich again, Meena, what do you say?'

Meena, as usual, said nothing; but took Kapoor by the arm and bundled him out of the shop and into the car.

'Be quick with the chaat shop!' cried Kapoor.

'I will have it in the house in five minutes,' called Rusty. 'Get everything ready!'

He returned to Kishen, who was stuffing himself with chaat; his father's behaviour did not appear to have affected him, he was unconscious of its ridiculous aspect and felt no shame; he was unconscious too of the considerate manner of the chaat-wallah, who felt sorry for the neglected child. The chaat-wallah did not know that Kishen enjoyed being neglected.

Rusty said, 'Come, let's go . . .'

'What's the hurry, Rusty? Sit down and eat, there's plenty of dough tonight. At least give Mummy time to put the sleeping tablets in the whisky.'

So they sat and ate their fill, and listened to other people's gossip; then Kishen suggested that they explore the bazaar.

The oil lamps were lit, and the main road bright and crowded; but Kishen and Rusty went down an alleyway, where the smells were more complicated and the noise intermittent; two women spoke to each other from their windows on either side of the road, a baby cried monoton-ously, a cheap gramophone blared. Kishen and Rusty walked aimlessly through the maze of alleyways.

'Why are you white like Suri?' asked Kishen.

'Why is Suri white?'

'He is Kashmiri; they are fair.'

'Well, I am English . . .'

'English?' said Kishen disbelievingly. 'You? But you do not look like one.'

Rusty hesitated: he did not feel there was any point in raking up a past that was as much a mystery to him as it was to Kishen.

'I don't know,' he said. 'I never saw my parents. And I don't care what they were and I don't care what I am, and I'm not very interested . . .'

But he couldn't help wondering, and Kishen couldn't help wondering, so they walked on in silence, wondering . . . They reached the railway station, which was at the end of the bazaar; the gates were closed, but they peered through the railings at the goods wagons. A pleasure house did business near the station.

'If you want to have fun,' said Kishen, 'let's climb that roof. From the skylight you can see everything.'

'No fun in just watching,' said Rusty.

'Have you ever watched?'

'Of course,' lied Rusty, turning homewards; he walked with a distracted air.

'What are you thinking of?' asked Kishen.

'Nothing.'

'You must be in love.'

'That's right.'

'Who is it, eh?'

'If I told you,' said Rusty, 'you'd be jealous.'

'But I'm not in love with anybody. Come on, tell me, I'm your friend.'

'Would you be angry if I said I loved your mother?'

'Mummy!' exclaimed Kishen. 'But she's old! She's married. Hell, who would think of falling in love with Mummy? Don't joke, mister.'

'I'm sorry,' said Rusty.

They walked on in silence and crossed the maidan, leaving the bazaar behind. It was dark on the maidan, they could hardly see each other's faces; Kishen put his hand on Rusty's shoulder.

'If you love her,' he said, 'I'm not jealous. But it sounds funny . . .'

Chapter Twelve

In his room, Rusty was a king. His domain was the sky and everything he could see. His subjects were the people who passed below, but they were his subjects only while they were below and he was on the roof; and he spied on them through the branches of the banyan tree. His close confidants were the inhabitants of the banyan tree; which, of course, included Kishen.

It was the day of the picnic, and Rusty had just finished bathing at the water tank. He had become used to the people at the tank and had made friends with the ayahs and their charges. He had come to like their bangles and bracelets and ankle-bells. He liked to watch one of them at the tap, squatting on her haunches, scrubbing her feet, and making much music with the bells and bangles; she would roll her sari up to the knees to give her legs greater freedom, and crouch forward so that her jacket revealed a modest expanse of waist.

It was the day of the picnic, and Rusty had bathed, and now he sat on a disused chimney, drying himself in the sun.

Summer was coming. The litchees were almost ready to eat, the mangoes ripened under Kishen's greedy eye. In the afternoons, the sleepy sunlight stole through the branches of the banyan tree and made a patchwork of arched shadows on the walls of the house. The inhabitants of the trees knew that summer was coming; Somi's slippers knew it, and slapped lazily against his heels; and Kishen grumbled and became more untidy, and even Suri seemed to be taking a rest from his private investigations. Yes, summer was coming.

And it was the day of the picnic.

The car had been inspected, and the two bottles that Kapoor had hidden in the dicky had been found and removed; Kapoor was put into khaki drill trousers and a bush-shirt and pronounced fit to drive; a basket of food and a gramophone were in the dicky. Suri had a camera slung over his shoulders; Kishen was sporting a Gurkha hat; and Rusty had on a thick leather belt reinforced with steel knobs. Meena had dressed in a hurry, and looked the better for it. And for once, Somi had tied his turban to perfection.

'Everyone present?' said Meena. 'If so, get into the car.'

'I'm waiting for my dog,' said Suri, and he had hardly made the announcement when from around the corner came a yapping mongrel.

'He's called Prickly Heat,' said Suri. 'We'll put him in the back seat.'

'He'll go in the dicky,' said Kishen. 'I can see the lice from here.'

Prickly Heat wasn't any particular kind of dog, just a kind of dog; he hadn't even the stump of a tail. But he had sharp, pointed ears that wagged as well as any tail, and they were working furiously this morning.

Suri and the dog were both deposited in the dicky; Somi, Kishen and Rusty made themselves comfortable in the back seat; and Meena sat next to her husband in the front. The car belched and lurched forward, and stirred up great clouds of dust; then, accelerating, sped out of the compound and across the narrow wooden bridge that spanned the canal.

The sun rose over the forest, and a spiral of smoke from a panting train was caught by a slanting ray and spangled with gold. The air was fresh and exciting. It was ten miles to the river and the sulphur springs, ten miles of intermittent grumbling and gaiety, with Prickly Heat yapping in the dicky and Kapoor whistling at the wheel and Kishen letting fly from the window with a catapult.

Somi said: 'Rusty, your pimples will leave you if you bathe in the sulphur springs.'

'I would rather have pimples than pneumonia,' replied Rusty.

'But it's not cold,' and Kishen. 'I would bathe myself, but I don't feel very well.'

'Then you shouldn't have come,' said Meena from the front.

'I didn't want to disappoint you all,' said Kishen.

Before reaching the springs, the car had to cross one or two riverbeds, usually dry at this time of the year. But the mountains had tricked the party, for there was a good deal of water to be seen, and the current was strong.

'It's not very deep,' said Kapoor, at the first riverbed, 'I think we can drive through easily.'

The car dipped forward, rolled down the bank, and entered the current with a great splash. In the dicky, Suri got a soaking.

'Got to go fast,' said Kapoor, 'or we'll stick.'

He accelerated, and a great spray of water rose on both

sides of the car. Kishen cried out for sheer joy, but at the back, Suri was having a fit of hysterics.

'I think the dog's fallen out,' said Meena.

'Good,' said Somi.

'I think Suri's fallen out,' said Rusty.

'Good,' said Somi.

Suddenly the engines spluttered and choked, and the car came to a standstill.

'We have stuck,' said Kapoor.

'That,' said Meena bitingly, 'is obvious. Now I suppose you want us all to get out and push?'

'Yes, that's a good idea.'

'You're a genius.'

Kishen had his shoes off in a flash, and was leaping about in the water with great abandon. The water reached up to his knees and, as he hadn't been swept off his feet, the others followed his example.

Meena rolled her sari up to the thighs, and stepped gingerly into the current. Her legs, so seldom exposed, were very fair in contrast to her feet and arms, but they were strong and nimble, and she held herself erect. Rusty stumbled to her side, intending to aid her; but ended by clinging to her dress for support. Suri was not to be seen anywhere.

'Where is Suri?' said Meena.

'Here,' said a muffled voice from the floor of the dicky. 'I've got sick. I can't push.'

'All right,' said Meena. 'But you'll clean up the mess yourself.'

Somi and Kishen were looking for fish. Kapoor tootled the horn.

'Are you all going to push?' he said. 'Or are we going to have the picnic in the middle of the river?'

Rusty was surprised at Kapoor's unusual display of common sense; when sober, Kapoor did sometimes have moments of sanity.

Everyone put their weight against the car, and pushed with all their strength; and, as the car moved slowly forward, Rusty felt a thrill of health and pleasure run through his body. In front of him, Meena pushed silently, the muscles of her thighs trembling with the strain. They all pushed silently, with determination; the sweat ran down Somi's face and neck, and Kishen's jaws worked desperately on his chewing gum. But Kapoor sat in comfort behind the wheel, pressing and pulling knobs, and saying 'harder, push harder', and Suri began to be sick again. Prickly Heat was strangely quiet, and it was assumed that the dog was sick too.

With one last final heave, the car was moved up the

opposite bank and on to the straight. Everyone groaned and flopped to the ground. Meena's hands were trembling.

'You shouldn't have pushed,' said Rusty.

'I enjoyed it,' she said, smiling at him. 'Help me to get up.'

He rose and, taking her hand, pulled her to her feet. They stood together, holding hands. Kapoor fiddled around with starters and chokes and things.

'It won't go,' he said. 'I'll have to look at the engine. We might as well have the picnic here.'

So out came the food and lemonade bottles and, miraculously enough, out came Suri and Prickly Heat, looking as fit as ever.

'Hey,' said Kishen, 'we thought you were sick. I suppose you were just making room for lunch.'

'Before he eats anything,' said Somi, 'he's going to get wet. Let's take him for a swim.'

Somi, Kishen and Rusty caught hold of Suri and dragged him along the riverbank to a spot downstream where the current was mild and the water warm and waist-high. They unrobed Suri, took off their own clothes, and ran down the sandy slope to the water's edge; feet splashed ankle-deep, calves thrust into the current, and then the ground suddenly disappeared beneath their feet.

Somi was a fine swimmer; his supple limbs cut through

the water and, when he went under, he was almost as powerful; the chequered colours of his body could be seen first here and then there, twisting and turning, diving and disappearing for what seemed like several minutes, and then coming up under someone's feet.

Rusty and Kishen were amateurs. When they tried swimming underwater, their bottoms remained on the surface, having all the appearance of floating buoys. Suri couldn't swim at all but, though he was often out of his depth and frequently ducked, managed to avoid his death by drowning.

They heard Meena calling them for food, and scrambled up the bank, the dog yapping at their heels. They ate in the shade of a poinsettia tree, whose red long-fingered flowers dropped sensually to the running water; and when they had eaten, lay down to sleep or drowse the afternoon away.

When Rusty awoke, it was evening, and Kapoor was tinkering about with the car, muttering to himself, a little cross because he hadn't had a drink since the previous night. Somi and Kishen were back in the river, splashing away, and this time they had Prickly Heat for company. Suri wasn't in sight. Meena stood in a clearing at the edge of the forest.

Rusty went to Meena, but she wandered into the thicket.

The boy followed. She must have expected him, for she showed no surprise at his appearance.

'Listen to the jungle,' she said.

'I can't hear anything.'

'That's what I mean. Listen to nothing.'

They were surrounded by silence; a dark, pensive silence, heavy, scented with magnolia and jasmine.

It was shattered by a piercing shriek, a cry that rose on all sides, echoing against the vibrating air; and, instinctively, Rusty put his arm round Meena – whether to protect her or to protect himself, he did not really know – and held her tight.

'It is only a bird,' she said, 'of what are you afraid?'

But he was unable to release his hold, and she made no effort to free herself. She laughed into his face, and her eyes danced in the shadows. But he stifled her laugh with his lips.

It was a clumsy, awkward kiss, but fiercely passionate, and Meena responded, tightening the embrace, returning the fervour of the kiss. They stood together in the shadows, Rusty intoxicated with beauty and sweetness, Meena with freedom and the comfort of being loved.

A monkey chattered shrilly in a branch above them, and the spell was broken.

'Oh, Meena . . .'

'Shh . . . you spoil these things by saying them.'

'Oh, Meena . . .'

They kissed again, but the monkey set up such a racket that they feared it would bring Kapoor and the others to the spot. So they walked through the trees, holding hands.

They were barefooted, but they did not notice the thorns and brambles that pricked their feet; they walked through heavy foliage, nettles and long grass, until they came to a clearing and a stream.

Rusty was conscious of a wild urge, a desire to escape from the town and its people, and live in the forest with Meena, with no one but Meena . . .

As though conscious of his thoughts, she said: 'This is where we drink. In the trees we eat and sleep, and here we drink.'

She laughed, but Rusty had a dream in his heart. The pebbles on the bed of the stream were round and smooth, taking the flow of water without resistance. Only weed and rock could resist water; only weed or rock could resist life.

'It would be nice to stay in the jungle,' said Meena. 'Let us stay . . .'

'We will be found. We cannot escape – from – others . . .'

'Even the world is too small. Maybe there is more

freedom in your little room than in all the jungle and all the world.'

Rusty pointed to the stream and whispered, 'Look!'

Meena looked, and at the same time, a deer looked up. They looked at each other with startled, fascinated eyes, the deer and Meena. It was a spotted cheetal, a small animal with delicate, quivering limbs and muscles, and young green antlers.

Rusty and Meena did not move; nor did the deer; they might have gone on staring at each other all night if somewhere a twig hadn't snapped sharply.

At the snap of the twig, the deer jerked its head up with a start, lifted one foot pensively, sniffed the air; then leapt the stream and, in a single bound, disappeared into the forest.

The spell was broken, the magic lost. Only the water ran on and life ran on.

'Let's go back,' said Meena.

They walked back through the dappled sunlight, swinging their clasped hands like two children who had only just discovered love.

Their hands parted as they reached the riverbed.

Miraculously enough, Kapoor had started the car, and was waving his arms and shouting to everyone to come home. Everyone was ready to start back except for Suri and Prickly Heat, who were nowhere to be seen. Nothing, thought Meena, would have been better than for Suri to disappear forever, but unfortunately she had taken full responsibility for his well-being, and did not relish the thought of facing his strangely affectionate mother. So she asked Rusty to shout for him.

Rusty shouted, and Meena shouted, and Somi shouted, and then they all shouted together, only Suri didn't shout.

'He's up to his tricks,' said Kishen. 'We shouldn't have brought him. Let's pretend we're leaving, then he'll be scared.'

So Kapoor started the engine, and everyone got in, and it was only then that Suri came running from the forest, the dog at his heels, his shirt tails flapping in the breeze, his hair wedged between his eyes and his spectacles.

'Hey, wait for us!' he cried. 'Do you want me to die?'

Kishen mumbled in the affirmative, and swore quietly.

'We thought you were in the dicky,' said Rusty.

Suri and Prickly Heat climbed into the dicky, and at the same time the car entered the river with a determined splashing and churning of wheels, to emerge the victor.

Everyone cheered, and Somi gave Kapoor such an enthusiastic slap on the back that the pleased recipient nearly caught his head in the steering wheel.

It was dark now, and all that could be seen of the countryside was what the headlights showed. Rusty had hopes of seeing a panther or tiger, for this was their territory, but only a few goats blocked the road. However, for the benefit of Suri, Somi told a story of a party that had gone for an outing in a car and, on returning home, had found a panther in the dicky.

Kishen fell asleep just before they reached the outskirts of Dehra, his fuzzy head resting on Rusty's shoulder. Rusty felt protectively towards the boy, for a bond of genuine affection had grown between the two. Somi was Rusty's best friend, in the same way that Ranbir was a friend, and their friendship was on a high emotional plane. But Kishen was a brother more than a friend. He loved Rusty, but without knowing or thinking or saying it, and that is the love of a brother.

Somi began singing. Then the town came in sight, the bazaar lights twinkling defiance at the starry night.

Chapter Thirteen

Rusty and Mr Harrison met in front of the town's main grocery store, the 'wine and general merchant's'; it was part of the smart shopping centre, alien to the bazaar but far from the European community – and thus neutral ground for Rusty and Mr Harrison.

'Hullo, Mr Harrison,' said Rusty, confident of himself and deliberately omitting the customary 'sir'.

Mr Harrison tried to ignore the boy, but found him blocking the way to the car. Not wishing to lose his dignity, he decided to be pleasant.

'This is a surprise,' he said, 'I never thought I'd see you again.'

'I found a job,' said Rusty, taking the opportunity of showing his independence. 'I meant to come and see you, but didn't get the time.'

'You're always welcome. The missionary's wife often

speaks of you, she'd be glad to see you. By the way, what's your job?'

Rusty hesitated; he did not know how his guardian would take the truth – probably with a laugh or a sneer ('you're *teaching*!') – and decided to be mysterious about his activities.

'Babysitting,' he replied, with a disarming smile. 'Anyway, I'm not starving. And I've got many friends.'

Mr Harrison's face darkened, and the corners of his mouth twitched; but he remembered that times had changed, and that Rusty was older and also free, and that he wasn't in his own house; and he controlled his temper.

'I can get you a job,' he said. 'On a tea estate. Or, if you like to go abroad, I have friends in Guiana . . .'

'I like babysitting,' said Rusty.

Mr Harrison smiled, got into the car, and lit a cigarette before starting the engine. 'Well, as I said, you're always welcome in the house.'

'Thanks,' said Rusty. 'Give my regards to the sweeper boy.'

The atmosphere was getting tense.

'Why don't you come and see him some time?' said Mr Harrison, as softly and as malevolently as he could.

It was just as well the engine had started.

'I will,' said Rusty.'

'I kicked him out,' said Mr Harrison, putting his foot down on the accelerator and leaving Rusty in a cloud of dust.

But Rusty's rage turned to pleasure when the car almost collided with a stationary bullock cart, and a uniformed policeman brought it to a halt. With the feeling that he had been the master of the situation, Rusty walked homewards.

The litchee trees were covered with their pink-skinned fruit and the mangoes were almost ripe. The mango is a passionate fruit, its inner gold sensuous to the lips and tongue. The grass had not yet made up its mind to remain yellow or turn green, and would probably keep its dirty colour until the monsoon rains arrived.

Meena met Rusty under the banana trees.

'I am bored,' she said, 'so I am going to give you a haircut. Do you mind?'

'I will do anything to please you. But don't take it all off.'

'Don't you trust me?'

'I love you.'

Rusty was wrapped up in a sheet and placed on a chair. He looked up at Meena, and their eyes met, laughing, blue and brown.

Meena cut silently, and the fair hair fell quickly, softly, lightly to the ground. Rusty enjoyed the snip of the scissors and the sensation of lightness; it was as though his mind was being given more room in which to explore.

Kishen came loafing around the corner of the house, still wearing his pyjamas, which were rolled up to the knees. When he saw what was going on, he burst into laughter.

'And what is so funny?' said Rusty.

'You!' spluttered Kishen. 'Where is your hair, your beautiful golden hair? Has Mummy made you become a monk? Or have you got ringworm? Or fleas? Look at the ground, all that beautiful hair!'

'Don't be funny, Kishen bhaiya,' said Meena, 'or you will get the same treatment.'

'Is it so bad?' asked Rusty anxiously.

'Don't you trust me?' said Meena.

'I love you.'

Meena glanced swiftly at Kishen to see if he had heard the last remark, but he was still laughing at Rusty's haircut and prodding his nose for all he was worth.

'Rusty, I have a favour to ask you,' said Meena. 'Kapoor and I may be going to Delhi for a few weeks, as there is a chance of him getting a good job. We are not taking

Kishen bhaiya, as he is only nuisance value, so will you look after him and keep him out of mischief? I will leave some money with you. About how much will you need for two weeks?'

'When are you going?' asked Rusty, already in the depths of despair.

'How much will you need?'

'Oh, fifty rupees . . . but when –'

'A hundred rupees!' interrupted Kishen. 'Oh boy, Rusty, we'll have fun!'

'Seventy-five,' said Meena, as though driving a bargain, 'and I'll send more after two weeks. But we should be back by then. There, Rusty, your haircut is complete.'

But Rusty wasn't interested in the result of the haircut; he felt like sulking; he wanted to have some say in Meena's plans, he felt he had a right to a little power.

That evening, in the front room, he didn't talk much. Nobody spoke. Kishen lay on the ground, stroking his stomach, his toes tracing imaginary patterns on the wall. Meena looked tired; wisps of hair had fallen across her face, and she did not bother to brush them back. She took Kishen's foot and gave it a pull.

'Go to bed,' she said.

'Not tired.'

'Go to bed, or you'll get a slap.'

Kishen laughed defiantly, but got up from the floor and ambled out of the room.

'And don't wake Daddy,' she said.

Kapoor had been put to bed early, as Meena wanted him to be fresh and sober for his journey to Delhi and his interviews there. But every now and then he would wake up and call out for something – something unnecessary, so that after a while no one paid any attention to his requests. He was like an irritable invalid, to be humoured and tolerated.

'Are you not feeling well, Meena?' asked Rusty. 'If you like, I'll also go.'

'I am only tired, don't go . . .'

She went to the window and drew the curtains and put out the light. Only the table lamp burned. The lampshade was decorated with dragons and butterflies – it was a Chinese lampshade – and, as Rusty sat gazing at the light, the dragons began to move and the butterflies flutter. He couldn't see Meena, but felt her presence across the room.

She turned from the window; and silently, with hardly a rustle, slipped to the ground. Her back against the couch, her head resting against the cushion, she looked up at the ceiling. Neither of them spoke.

From the next room came sounds of Kishen preparing for the night, one or two thumps and a muttered imprecation. Kapoor snored quietly to himself, and the rest was silence.

Rusty's gaze left the revolving dragons and prancing butterflies to settle on Meena, who sat still and tired, her feet lifeless against the table legs, her slippers fallen to the ground. In the lamplight, her feet were like jade.

A moth began to fly round the lamp, and it went round and round and closer, till – with a sudden plop – it hit the lampshade and fell to the ground. But Rusty and Meena were still silent, their breathing the only conversation.

Chapter Fourteen

During the day, flies circled the room with feverish buzzing, and at night the mosquitoes came singing in one's ears; summer days were hot and sticky, the nights breathless.

Rusty covered his body in citronella oil, which had been given him by Somi's mother; its smell, while pleasant to his own senses, was repugnant to mosquitoes.

When Rusty rubbed the oil on his limbs he noticed the change in his physique. He had lost his puppy fat, and there was more muscle to his body; his complexion was a healthier colour, and his pimples had almost disappeared. Nearly everyone had advised him about his pimples: drink *dahi*, said Somi's mother, don't eat fat; eat carrots, said Somi; plenty of fruit – mangoes! said Kishen; not at all, oranges; see a doctor, said Meena; have a whisky, said

Kapoor: but the pimples disappeared without any of these remedies, and Rusty put it down to his falling in love.

The bougainvillea creeper had advanced further into the room, and was now in flower; and watching Rusty oil himself was the bald maina bird; it had been in so many fights that the feathers on its head never got a chance to grow.

Suri entered the room without warning and, wiping his spectacles on the bed sheet, said: 'I have written an essay, Mister Rusty, for which I am going to be marked in school. Correct it, if you please.'

'Let me finish with this oil . . . It would be cheating, you know.'

'No, it won't. It has to be corrected some time, so you will save the master some trouble. Anyway, I'm leaving this rotten school soon. I'm going to Mussoorie.'

'To the same place as Ranbir? He'll be glad to see you.'

Suri handed Rusty the copy-book. On the cover was a pencil sketch of a rather overdeveloped nude.

'Don't tell me this is your school book!' exclaimed Rusty.

'No, only rough work.'

'You drew the picture?'

'Of course, don't you like it?'

'Did you copy it, or imagine it, or did someone pose for you?'

Suri winked. 'Someone posed.'

'You're a liar. And a pig.'

'Oh, look who's talking! You're not such a saint yourself, Mister Rusty.'

'Just what do you mean?' said Rusty, getting between Suri and the door.

'I mean, how is Mrs Kapoor, eh?'

'She is fine.'

'You get on well with her, eh?'

'We get on fine.'

'Like at the picnic?'

Suri rubbed his hands together, and smiled beatifically.

Rusty was momentarily alarmed. 'What do you mean, the picnic?'

'What did you do together, Mister Rusty, you and Mrs Kapoor? What happened in the bushes?'

Rusty leant against the wall, and returned Suri's smile, and said: 'I'll tell you what we did, my friend. There's nothing to hide between friends, is there? Well, Mrs Kapoor and I spent all our time making love. We did nothing but love each other. All the time. And Kapoor only a hundred yards away, and you in the next bush . . . Now what else do you want to know?'

Suri's smile was fixed. 'What if I tell Kapoor?'

'You won't tell him,' said Rusty.

'Why not?'

'Because you are the last person he'll believe. And you'll probably get a kick in the pants for the trouble.'

Suri's smile had gone.

'Cheer up,' said Rusty. 'What about the essay, do you want me to correct it?'

That afternoon the old car stood beneath the banana trees with an impatient driver tooting on the horn. The dicky and bumpers were piled high with tin trunks and bedding rolls, as though the Kapoors were going away for a lifetime. Meena wasn't going to let Kapoor drive her all the way to Delhi, and had taken on a professional instead.

Kapoor sat on the steps of the house, wearing his green dressing gown, and making a throaty noise similar to that of the motor horn.

'The devil!' he exclaimed, gesticulating towards Meena, who was bustling about indoors. 'The devil of a wife is taking me to Delhi! Ha! The car will never get there.'

'Oh yes, it will,' said Meena, thrusting her head out of the window, 'and it will get there with you in it, whether or not you shave and dress. So you might as well take a seat from now.'

Rusty went into the house, and found Meena locking rooms.

She was looking a little tired and irritable.

'You're going sooner than I expected,' said Rusty. 'Has Kishen got the money?'

'No, you must keep it. I'll give it to you in five rupee notes, wait a minute . . . He'll have to sleep with you, I'm locking the house . . .'

She opened a drawer and, taking out an envelope, gave it to Rusty.

'The money,' she said. Rusty picked up a small suitcase and followed Meena outside to the car. He waited until she was seated before handing her the case and, when he did, their hands touched. She laced her fingers with his, and gave him a quick smile, and squeezed his fingers.

From the front seat Kapoor beckoned Rusty. He grasped the boy's hand, and slipped a key into it.

'My friend,' he whispered, 'these are the keys of the back door. In the kitchen you will find six bottles of whisky. Keep them safe, until our return.'

Rusty shook Kapoor's hand, the hand of the man he laughed at, but whom he could not help loving as well.

In the confusion Kishen had gone almost unnoticed, but he was there all the time, and now he suffered a light kiss from his mother and a heavy one from his father.

The car belched and, after narrowly missing a banana tree, rattled down the gravel path, bounced over a ditch, and disappeared in a cloud of dust.

Kishen and Rusty were flapping their handkerchiefs for all they were worth. Kishen was not a bit sorry that his parents had gone away, but Rusty felt like crying. He was conscious now of a sense of responsibility, which was a thing he did not like having, and of a sense of loss. But the depression was only momentary.

'Hey!' said Kishen. 'Do you see what I see?'

'I can see a lot of things that you can see, so what do you mean?'

'The clothes! Mummy's washing, it is all on the rose bushes!' Meena had left without collecting her washing which, as always, had been left to dry on the rose bushes. Kapoor's underwear spread itself over an entire bush, and another tree was decorated with bodices and blouses of all colours.

Rusty said: 'Perhaps she means them to dry by the time she comes back.'

He began to laugh with Kishen, so it was a good thing, Meena's forgetfulness; it softened the pain of parting.

'What if we hadn't noticed?' chuckled Kishen.

'They would have been stolen.'

'Then we must reward ourselves. What about the chaat shop, bhai?'

At the risk of making himself unpopular, Rusty faced Kishen and, with a determination, said: 'No chaat shop. We have got seventy rupees to last a month, and I am not going to write for more once this finishes. We are having our meals with Somi. So, bhai, no chaat shop!'

'You are a swine, Rusty.'

'And the same to you.'

In this endearing mood they collected the clothes from the rose bushes, and marched upstairs to the room on the roof.

There was only one bed, and Kishen was a selfish sleeper; twice during the night Rusty found himself on the floor. Eventually he sat in the chair, with his feet on the table, and stared out of the window at the black night. Even if he had been comfortable, he would not have slept; he felt terribly lovesick. He wanted to write a poem, but it was too dark to write; he wanted to write a letter, but she hadn't been away a day; he wanted to run away with Meena, into the hills, into the forests, where no one could find them, and he wanted to be with her forever and never grow old ... neither of them must ever grow old ...

Chapter Fifteen

In the morning there was a note from Suri. Rusty wondered how Suri had managed to leave it on the doorstep without being seen. It went:

Tomorrow I'm going up to Mussoorie. This is to request the pleasure of Misters Rusty and Kishen to my goodbye party, five o'clock sharp this same evening.

As soon as it became known that Suri was leaving, everyone began to love him. And everyone brought him presents, just so he wouldn't change his mind and stay.

Kishen bought him a pair of cheap binoculars so that he could look at the girls more closely, and the guests sat down at a table and Suri entertained them in grand style; and they tolerated everything he said and were particularly friendly and gave him three cheers, hooray, hooray, hooray, they were so glad he was going.

They drank lemonade and ate cream cakes (especially obtained from the smart restaurant amongst the smart shops) and Kishen said, 'We are so sorry you are leaving, Suri,' and they had more cream cakes and lemonade, and Kishen said, 'You are like a brother to us, Suri dear'; and when the cream cakes had all been finished, Kishen fell on Suri's neck and kissed him.

It was all very moving, those cream cakes and lemonade and Suri going away.

Kishen made himself sick, and Rusty had to help him back to the room. Kishen lay prostrate on the bed, whilst Rusty sat in front of the window, gazing blankly into the branches of the banyan tree.

Presently he said: 'It's drizzling. I think there'll be a storm, I've never seen the sky so black.'

As though to confirm this observation, there was a flash of lightning in the sky. Rusty's eyes lit up with excitement; he liked storms; sometimes they were an expression of his innermost feelings.

'Shut the window,' said Kishen.

'If I shut the window, I will kill the flowers on the creeper.'

Kishen snorted, 'You're a poet, that's what you are!'

'One day I'll write poems.'

'Why not today?'

'Too much is happening today.'

'I don't think so. Nothing ever happens in Dehra. The place is dead. Why don't you start writing now? You're a great writer, I told you so before.'

'I know.'

'One day . . . one day you'll be a king . . . but only in your dreams . . . Meanwhile, shut the window!'

But Rusty liked the window open, he liked the rain flecking his face, and he liked to watch it pattering on the leaves of the banyan tree.

'They must have reached Delhi now,' he said, half to himself.

'Daddy's drunk,' said Kishen.

'There's nothing for him to drink'

'Oh, he'll find something. You know, one day he drank up all the hair oil in the house. Hey, didn't he give you the keys of the back door? Let's drink one of the bottles ourselves . . .'

Rusty didn't reply. The tense sky shuddered. The blanket of black cloud groaned aloud and the air, which had been still and sultry, trembled with electricity. Then the thunder gave a great clap, and all at once the hailstones came clattering down on the corrugated iron roof.

'What a noise!' exclaimed Kishen. 'You'd think a lot of skeletons were having a fight on the roof!'

The hailstones, as big as marbles, bounced in from the doorway, and on the roof they were forming a layer of white ice. Through the window Rusty could see one of the ayahs tearing down the gravel path, the pram bouncing madly over the stones, the end of her head cloth flapping wildly.

'Will you shut the window!' screamed Kishen.

'Why are you so cruel, bhai?'

'I'm not cruel, I'm *sick*! Do you want me to get sick all over the place?'

As gently as he could, Rusty pushed the creeper out of the window and laid it against the outside wall. Then he closed the window. This shut out the view, because the window was made of plywood and had no glass panes.

'And the door,' moaned Kishen.

With the door closed, the room was plunged into darkness.

'What a room,' complained Kishen, 'not even a light. You'll have to live downstairs when they come back.'

'But I like it here.'

The storm continued all night; it made Kishen so

nervous that, instead of pushing Rusty off the bed, he put his arms round him for protection.

The rain had stopped by morning, but the sky was still overcast and threatening. Rusty and Kishen lay in bed, too bored to bestir themselves. There was some dried fruit in a tin, and they ate the nuts continuously. They could hear the postman making his rounds below, and Rusty suddenly remembered that the postman wouldn't know the Kapoors had left. He leapt out of bed, opened the door, and ran to the edge of the roof.

'Hey, postman!' he called. 'Anything for Mr and Mrs Kapoor?'

'Nothing,' said the postman, 'but there is something for you, shall I come up?'

But Rusty was already on his way down, certain that it was a letter from Meena.

It was a telegram. Rusty's fingers trembled as he tore it open, and he had read it before he reached the room. His face was white when he entered the room.

'What's wrong,' said Kishen, 'you look sick. Doesn't Mummy love you any more?'

Rusty sat down on the edge of the bed, his eyes staring emptily at the floor.

'You're to go to Hardwar,' he said at last, 'to stay with your aunty.'

'Well, you can tell Mummy I'm staying here.'

'It's from your aunty.'

'Why couldn't Mummy say so herself?'

'I don't want to tell you.'

'But you have to tell me!' cried Kishen, making an ineffectual grab at the telegram. 'You have to tell me, Rusty, you have to!'

There was panic in Kishen's voice, he was almost hysterical.

'All right,' said Rusty, and his own voice was strained and hollow. 'The car had an accident.'

'And something happened to Daddy?'

'No.'

There was a terrible silence. Kishen looked helplessly at Rusty, his eyes full of tears and bewilderment; and Rusty could stand the strain no longer, and threw his arms round Kishen, and wept uncontrollably.

'Oh, Mummy, Mummy,' cried Kishen. 'Oh, Mummy . . .'

Chapter Sixteen

It was late evening the same day, and the clouds had passed and the whole sky was sprinkled with stars. Rusty sat on the bed, looking out at the stars and waiting for Kishen.

Presently bare feet sounded on the stone floor, and Rusty could make out the sharp lines of Kishen's body against the faint moon in the doorway.

'Why do you creep in like a ghost?' whispered Rusty.

'So's not to wake you.'

'It's still early. Where have you been, I was looking for you.'

'Oh, just walking . . .'

Kishen sat down beside Rusty, facing the same way, the stars. The moonlight ran over their feet, but their faces were in darkness.

'Rusty,' said Kishen.

'Yes.'

'I don't want to go to Hardwar.'

'I know you don't, bhaiya. But you will not be allowed to stay here. You must go to your relatives. And Hardwar is a beautiful place, and people are kind . . .'

'I'll stay with you.'

'I can't look after you, Kishen, I haven't got any money, any work . . . you must stay with your aunt. I'll come to see you.'

'You'll never come.'

'I'll try.'

Every night the jackals could be heard howling in the nearby jungle, but tonight their cries sounded nearer, much nearer the house. Kishen slept. He was exhausted; he had been walking all evening, crying his heart out. Rusty lay awake; his eyes were wide open, brimming with tears; he did not know if the tears were for himself or for Meena or for Kishen, but they were for someone.

Meena is dead, he told himself, Meena is dead; if there is a god, then God look after her; if God is Love, then my love will be with her; she loved me; I can see her so clearly, her face speckled with sun and shadow when we kissed in the forest, the black waterfall of hair, her tired eyes, her feet like jade in the lamplight, she loved me, she was mine . . .

Rusty was overcome by a feeling of impotence and futility, and of the unimportance of life. Every moment, he told himself, every moment someone is born and someone dies, you can count them, one, two, three, a birth and a death for every moment . . . what is this one life in the whole pattern of life, what is this one death but a passing of time . . . And if I were to die now, suddenly and without cause, what would happen, would it matter . . . we live without knowing why or to what purpose.

The moon bathed the room in a soft, clear light. The howl of the jackals seemed to be coming from the field below, and Rusty thought, *A jackal is like death, ugly and cowardly and mad* . . . He heard a faint sniff from the doorway and lifted his head.

In the doorway, a dark silhouette against the moonlight, stood the lean, craving form of a jackal, its eyes glittering balefully.

Rusty wanted to scream. He wanted to throw everything in the room at the snivelling, cold-blooded beast, or throw himself out of the window instead. But he could do none of these things.

The jackal lifted its head to the sky and emitted a long, blood-curdling howl that ran like an electric current through Rusty's body. Kishen sprang up with a gasp and threw his arms round Rusty.

And then Rusty screamed.

It was half shout, half scream, and it began in the pit of his stomach, was caught by his lungs, and catapulted into the empty night. Everything around him seemed to be shaking, vibrating to the pitch of the scream.

The jackal fled. Kishen whimpered and sprang back from Rusty and dived beneath the bedclothes.

And as the scream and its echo died away, the night closed in again, with a heavy, petrifying stillness; and all that could be heard was Kishen sobbing under the blankets, terrified not so much by the jackal's howl as by Rusty's own terrible scream.

'Oh, Kishen bhai,' cried Rusty, putting his arms around the boy, 'don't cry, please don't cry. You are making me afraid of myself. Don't be afraid, Kishen. Don't make me afraid of myself...'

And in the morning their relationship was a little strained.

Kishen's aunt arrived. She had a tonga ready to take Kishen away. She give Rusty a hundred rupees, which she said was from Kapoor; Rusty didn't want to take it, but Kishen swore at him and forced him to accept it.

The tonga pony was restless, pawing the ground and champing at the bit, snorting a little. The driver got down from the carriage and held the reins whilst Kishen and his aunt climbed on to their seats.

Kishen made no effort to conceal his misery. 'I wish you would come, Rusty,' he said.

'I will come and see you one day, be sure of that.'

It was very seldom that Kishen expressed any great depth of feeling; he was always so absorbed with comforts of the flesh that he never had any profound thoughts; but he did have profound feelings, though they were seldom thought or spoken.

He grimaced and prodded his nose. 'Inside of me,' he said, 'I am all lonely . . .'

The driver cracked his whip, the horse snorted, the wheels creaked, and the tonga moved forward. The carriage bumped up in the ditch, and it looked as though everyone would be thrown out; but it bumped down again without falling apart, and Kishen and his aunt were still in their seats. The driver jingled his bell, and the tonga turned on to the main road that led to the station; the horse's hoofs clip-clopped, and the carriage wheels squeaked and rattled.

Rusty waved. Kishen sat stiff and upright, clenching the ends of his shirt.

Rusty felt afraid for Kishen, who seemed to be sitting on his own, apart from his aunt, as though he disowned or did not know her: it seemed as though he were being borne away to some strange, friendless world, where no one would know or care for him; and, though Rusty knew Kishen to be wild and independent, he felt afraid for him.

The driver called to the horse, and the tonga went round the bend in the road and was lost to sight.

Rusty stood at the gate, staring down the empty road. He thought: *I'll go back to my room and time will run on and things will happen but this will not happen again . . . there will still be sun and litchees, and there will be other friends, but there will be no Meena and no Kishen, for our lives have drifted apart . . . Kishen and I have been going down the river together, but I have been caught in the reeds and he has been swept onwards; and if I do catch up with him, it will not be the same, it might be sad . . . Kishen has gone, and part of my life has gone with him, and inside of me, I am all lonely.*

Chapter Seventeen

It was a sticky, restless afternoon. The water-carrier passed below the room with his skin bag, spraying water on the dusty path. The toy seller entered the compound, calling his wares in a high-pitched sing-song voice, and presently there was the chatter of children.

The toy seller had a long bamboo pole, crossed by two or three shorter bamboos, from which hung all manner of toys – little celluloid drums, tin watches, tiny flutes and whistles, and multicoloured rag dolls – and when these ran out, they were replaced by others from a large bag, a most mysterious and fascinating bag, one in which no one but the toy seller was allowed to look. He was a popular person with rich and poor alike, for his toys never cost more than four annas and never lasted longer than a day.

Rusty liked the cheap toys, and was fond of decorating

the room with them. He bought a two-anna flute; and walked upstairs, blowing on it.

He removed his shirt and sandals and lay flat on the bed, staring up at the ceiling. The lizards scuttled along the rafters, the bald maina hopped along the window ledge. He was about to fall asleep when Somi came into the room.

Somi looked listless.

'I feel sticky,' he said, 'I don't want to wear any clothes.'

He too pulled off his shirt and deposited it on the table, then stood before the mirror, studying his physique. Then he turned to Rusty.

'You don't look well,' he said, 'there are cobwebs in your hair.'

'I don't care.'

'You must have been very fond of Mrs Kapoor. She was very kind.'

'I loved her, didn't you know?'

'No. My own love is the only thing I know. Rusty, best favourite friend, you cannot stay here in this room, you must come back to my house. Besides, this building will soon have new tenants.'

'I'll get out when they come, or when the landlord discovers I'm living here.'

Somi's usually bright face was somewhat morose, and there was a faint agitation showing in his eyes.

'I will go and get a cucumber to eat,' he said, 'then there is something to tell you.'

'I don't want a cucumber,' said Rusty, 'I want a coconut.'

'I want a cucumber.'

Rusty felt irritable. The room was hot, the bed was hot, his blood was hot. Impatiently, he said: 'Go and eat your cucumber, I don't want any . . .'

Somi looked at him with a pained surprise; then, without a word, picked up his shirt and marched out of the room. Rusty could hear the slap of his slippers on the stairs, and then the bicycle tyres on the gravel path.

'Hey, Somi!' shouted Rusty, leaping off the bed and running out on to the roof. 'Come back!'

But the bicycle jumped over the ditch, and Somi's shirt flapped, and there was nothing Rusty could do but return to bed. He was alarmed at his liverish ill-temper. He lay down again and stared at the ceiling, at the lizards chasing each other across the rafters. On the roof two crows were fighting, knocking each other's feathers out. Everyone was in a temper.

What's wrong? wondered Rusty. *I spoke to Somi in fever, not in anger, but my words were angry. Now I am miserable, fed up. Oh, hell . . .*

He closed his eyes and shut out everything.

He opened his eyes to laughter. Somi's face was close, laughing into Rusty's.

'Of what were you dreaming, Rusty, I have never seen you smile so sweetly!'

'Oh, I wasn't dreaming,' said Rusty, sitting up, and feeling better now that Somi had returned. 'I am sorry for being so grumpy, but I'm not feeling . . .'

'Quiet!' admonished Somi, putting his finger to the other's lips. 'See, I have settled the matter. Here is a coconut for you, and here is a cucumber for me!'

They sat cross-legged on the bed, facing each other: Somi with his cucumber, and Rusty with his coconut. The coconut milk trickled down Rusty's chin and on to his chest, giving him a cool, pleasant sensation.

Rusty said: 'I am afraid for Kishen. I am sure he will give trouble to his relatives, and they are not like his parents. Kapoor will have no say, without Meena.'

Somi was silent. The only sound was the munching of the cucumber and the coconut. He looked at Rusty, an uncertain smile on his lips but none in his eyes; and, in a forced conversational manner, said: 'I'm going to Amritsar for a few months. But I will be back in the spring, Rusty, you will be all right here . . .'

This news was so unexpected that for some time Rusty could not take it in. The thought had never occurred to him that one day Somi might leave Dehra, just as Ranbir and Suri and Kishen had done. He could not speak. A sickening heaviness clogged his heart and brain.

'Hey, Rusty!' laughed Somi. 'Don't look as though there is poison in the coconut!'

The poison lay in Somi's words. And the poison worked, running through Rusty's veins and beating against his heart and hammering on his brain. The poison worked, wounding him.

He said, 'Somi . . .' but could go no further.

'Finish the coconut!'

'Somi,' said Rusty again, 'if you are leaving Dehra, Somi, then I am leaving too.'

'Eat the coco . . . what did you say?'

'I am going too.'

'Are you mad?'

'Not at all.'

Serious now, and troubled, Somi put his hand on his friend's wrist; he shook his head, he could not understand.

'Why, Rusty? Where?'

'England.'

'But you haven't money, you silly fool!'

'I can get an assisted passage. The British Government will pay.'

'You are a British subject?'

'I don't know . . .'

'*Toba!*' Somi slapped his thighs and looked upwards in despair. 'You are neither Indian subject nor British subject, and you think someone is going to pay for your passage! And how are you to get a passport?

'How?' asked Rusty, anxious to find out.

'*Toba!* Have you a birth certificate?'

'Oh, no.'

'Then you are not born,' decreed Somi, with a certain amount of satisfaction. 'You are not alive! You do not happen to be in this world!'

He paused for breath, then waved his finger in the air. 'Rusty, you cannot go!' he said.

Rusty lay down despondently.

'I never really thought I would,' he said. 'I only said I would because I felt like it. Not because I am unhappy – I have never been happier elsewhere – but because I am restless as I have always been. I don't suppose I'll be anywhere for long . . .'

He spoke the truth. Rusty always spoke the truth. He defined truth as feeling, and when he said what he felt, he said truth. (Only he didn't always speak his feelings.) He never lied. You don't have to lie if you know how to withhold the truth.

'You belong here,' said Somi, trying to reconcile Rusty with circumstance. 'You will get lost in big cities, Rusty, you will break your heart. And when you come back – if you come back – I will be grown up and you will be grown up – I mean more than we are now – and we will be like strangers to each other . . . And besides, there are no chaat shops in England!'

'But I don't belong here, Somi. I don't belong anywhere. Even if I have papers, I don't belong. I'm a half-caste, I know it, and that is as good as not belonging anywhere.'

What am I saying, thought Rusty, *why do I make my inheritance a justification for my present bitterness? No one has cast me out . . . of my own free will I run away from India . . . why do I blame inheritance?*

'It can also mean that you belong everywhere,' said Somi. 'But you never told me. You are fair like a European.'

'I had not thought much about it.'

'Are you ashamed?'

'No. My guardian was. He kept it to himself, he only told me when I came home after playing Holi. I was happy then. So, when he told me, I was not ashamed, I was proud.'

'And now?'

'Now? Oh, I can't really believe it. Somehow I do not really feel mixed.'

'Then don't blame it for nothing.'

Rusty felt a little ashamed, and they were both silent awhile, then Somi shrugged and said: 'So you are going. You are running away from India.'

'No, not from India.'

'Then you are running away from your friends, from me!'

Rusty felt the irony of this remark, and allowed a tone of sarcasm into his voice.

'*You*, Master Somi, *you* are the one who is going away. I am still here. *You* are going to Amritsar. I only *want* to go. And I'm here alone; everyone has gone. So if I do eventually leave, the only person I'll be running away from will be myself!'

'Ah!' said Somi, nodding his head wisely. 'And by running away from yourself, you will be running away from me and from India! Now come on, let's go and have chaat.'

He pulled Rusty off the bed, and pushed him out of the room. Then, at the top of the steps, he leapt lightly on Rusty's back, kicked him with his heels, and shouted: 'Down the steps, my *tuttoo*, my pony! Fast down the steps!'

So Rusty carried him downstairs and dropped him on the grass. They laughed, but there was no great joy in their laughter; they laughed for the sake of friendship.

'Best favourite friend,' said Somi, throwing a handful of mud in Rusty's face.

Chapter Eighteen

Now everyone had gone from Dehra. Meena would never return; and it seemed unlikely that Kapoor could come back.

Kishen's departure was final. Ranbir would be in Mussoorie until the winter months, and this was still summer and it would be even longer before Somi returned. Everyone Rusty knew well had left, and there remained no one he knew well enough to love or hate. There were, of course, the people at the water tank – the servants, the ayahs, the babies – but they were busy all day. And when Rusty left them, he had no one but himself and memory for company.

He wanted to forget Meena. If Kishen had been with him, it would have been possible; the two boys would have found comfort in their companionship. But alone, Rusty realized he was not the master of himself.

And Kapoor. For Kapoor, Meena had died perfect. He suspected her of no infidelity. And, in a way, she had died perfect; for she had found a secret freedom. Rusty knew he had judged Kapoor correctly when scorning Suri's threat of blackmail; he knew Kapoor couldn't believe a single disparaging word about Meena.

And Rusty returned to his dreams, that wonderland of his, where he walked in perfection. He spoke to himself quite often, and sometimes he spoke to the lizards.

He was afraid of the lizards, afraid and at the same time fascinated. When they changed their colours, from brown to red to green, in keeping with their immediate surroundings, they fascinated him. But when they lost their grip on the ceiling and fell to the ground with a soft, wet, boneless smack, they repelled him. One night, he reasoned, one of them would most certainly fall on his face . . .

An idea he conceived one afternoon nearly sparked him into sudden and feverish activity. He thought of making a garden on the roof, beside his room.

The idea took his fancy to such an extent that he spent several hours planning the set-out of the flower beds, and visualizing the completed picture, with marigolds, zinnias and cosmos blooming everywhere. But there were no tools to be had, mud and bricks would have to be carried upstairs, seeds would have to be obtained; and, who knows, thought Rusty, after all that trouble the roof might cave in, or the rains might spoil everything . . . and anyway, he was going away . . .

His thoughts turned inwards. Gradually, he returned to the same frame of mind that had made life with his guardian so empty and meaningless; he began to fret, to dream, to lose his grip on reality. The full life of the past few months had suddenly ended, and the present was lonely and depressing; the future became a distorted image, created out of his own brooding fancies.

One evening, sitting on the steps, he found himself fingering a key. It was the key Kapoor had asked him to keep, the key to the back door. Rusty remembered the whisky bottles – 'let's drink them ourselves' Kishen had said – and Rusty thought, *Why not, why not . . . a few bottles can't do any harm . . .* and before he could have an argument with himself, the back door was open.

In his room that night he drank the whisky neat. It was the first time he had tasted alcohol, and he didn't find it pleasant; but he wasn't drinking for pleasure, he was drinking with the sole purpose of shutting himself off from the world and forgetting.

He hadn't drunk much when he observed that the roof had a definite slant; it seemed to slide away from his door to the field below, like a chute. The banyan tree was suddenly swarming with bees. The lizards were turning all colours at once, like pieces of rainbow.

When he had drunk a little more, he began to talk; not to himself any more, but to Meena, who was pressing his head and trying to force him down on the pillows. He struggled against Meena, but she was too powerful, and he began to cry.

Then he drank a little more. And now the floor began to wobble, and Rusty had a hard time keeping the table from toppling over. The walls of the room were caving in. He swallowed another mouthful of whisky, and held the wall up with his hands. He could deal with anything now. The bed was rocking, the chair was sliding about, the table was slipping, the walls were swaying, but Rusty had everything under control, he was everywhere at once, supporting the entire building with his bare hands.

And then he slipped, and everything came down on top of him, and it was black.

In the morning when he awoke, he threw the remaining bottles out of the window, and cursed himself for a fool, and went down to the water tank to bathe.

*

Days passed, dry and dusty, every day the same. Regularly, Rusty filled his earthen *sohrai* at the water tank, and soaked the reed mat that hung from the doorway. Sometimes, in the field, the children played cricket, but he couldn't summon up the energy to join them. From his room he could hear the sound of ball and bat, the shouting, the lone voice raised in shrill disagreement with some unfortunate umpire . . . or the thud of a football, or the clash of hockey sticks . . . but better than these sounds was the jingle of the bells and bangles on the feet of the ayahs, as they busied themselves at the water tank. Time passed, but Rusty did not know it was passing. It was like living in a house near a river, and the river was always running past the house, on and away; but to Rusty, living in the house, there was no passing of the river; the water ran on, the river remained.

He longed for something to happen.

Chapter Nineteen

Dust. It blew up in great clouds, swirling down the road, clutching and clinging to everything it touched; burning, choking, stinging dust.

Then thunder.

The wind dropped suddenly, there was a hushed expectancy in the air. And then, out of the dust, came big, black rumbling clouds.

Something was happening.

At first there was a lonely drop of water on the window sill; then a patter on the roof. Rusty felt a thrill of anticipation, and a mountain of excitement. The rains had come to break the monotony of the summer months; the monsoon had arrived!

The sky shuddered, the clouds groaned, a fork of lightning struck across the sky, and then the sky itself exploded.

The rain poured down, drumming on the corrugated roof. Rusty's vision was reduced to about twenty yards; it was as though the room had been cut off from the rest of the world by an impenetrable wall of water.

The rains had arrived, and Rusty wanted to experience to the full the novelty of that first shower. He threw off his clothes, and ran naked on to the roof, and the wind sprang up and whipped the water across his body so that he writhed in ecstasy. The rain was more intoxicating than the alcohol, and it was with difficulty that he restrained himself from shouting and dancing in mad abandon. The force and freshness of the rain brought tremendous relief, washed away the stagnation that had been settling on him, poisoning mind and body.

The rain swept over the town, cleansing the sky and earth. The trees bent beneath the force of wind and water. The field was a bog, flowers flattened to the ground.

Rusty returned to the room, exhilarated, his body weeping. He was confronted by a flood. The water had come in through the door and the window and the skylight, and the floor was flooded ankle-deep. He took to his bed.

The bed took on the glamour of a deserted island in the middle of the ocean. He dried himself on the sheets, conscious of a warm, sensuous glow. Then he sat on his haunches and gazed out through the window.

The rain thickened, the tempo quickened. There was the banging of a door, the swelling of a gutter, the staccato splutter of the rain rhythmically persistent on the roof. The drainpipe coughed and choked, the curtain flew to its limit; the lean trees swayed, swayed, bowed with the burden of wind and weather. The road was a rushing torrent, the gravel path inundated with little rivers. The monsoon had arrived!

But the rain stopped as unexpectedly as it had begun.

Suddenly it slackened, dwindled to a shower, petered out. Stillness. The dripping of water from the drainpipe drilled into the drain. Frogs croaked, hopping around in the slush.

The sun came out with a vengeance. On leaves and petals, drops of water sparkled like silver and gold. A cat emerged from a dry corner of the building, blinking sleepily, unperturbed and unenthusiastic.

The children came running out of their houses.

'*Barsaat, barsaat!*' they shouted. 'The rains have come!'

The rains had come. And the roof became a general bathing place. The children, the nightwatchmen, the dogs, all trouped up the steps to sample the novelty of a fresh-water shower on the roof. The maidan became alive with footballs. The game was called monsoon football; it was played in slush, in mud that was ankle-deep; and the football was heavy and slippery and difficult to kick with bare feet. The bazaar youths played barefooted because, in the first place, boots were too cumbersome for monsoon football, and in the second place they couldn't be afforded.

But the rains brought Rusty only a momentary elation, just as the first shower had seemed fiercer and fresher than those which followed; for now it rained every day . . .

Nothing could be more depressing than the dampness, the mildew, and the sunless heat that wrapped itself round the steaming land. Had Somi or Kishen been with Rusty, he might have derived some pleasure from the elements; had Ranbir been with him, he might have found adventure; but alone, he found only boredom.

He spent an idle hour watching the slow dripping from the pipe outside the door: where do I belong, he wondered, what am I doing, what is going to happen to me . . .

. . . He was determined to break away from the atmosphere of timelessness and resignation that surrounded him, and decided to leave Dehra.

'I must go,' he told himself. 'I do not want to rot like the mangoes at the end of the season, or burn out like the sun at the end of the day. I cannot live like the gardener, the cook and the water carrier, doing the same task every day of my life. I am not interested in today, I want tomorrow. I cannot live in this same small room all my life, with a family of lizards, living in other people's homes and never having one of my own. I *have* to break away. I want to be either somebody or nobody. I don't want to be anybody.'

He decided to go to Delhi and see the High Commissioner for the United Kingdom, who was sure to give him an assisted passage to England; and he wrote to Somi, telling him of this plan. On his way he would have to pass through Hardwar, and there he would see Kishen; he had the aunt's address.

At night he slept brokenly, thinking and worrying about the future. He would listen to the vibrant song of the frog who wallowed in the drain at the bottom of the steps, and to the unearthly cry of the jackal, and questions would come to him, disturbing questions about loving and leaving and living and dying, questions that crowded out his sleep.

But on the night before he left Dehra, it was not the croaking of the frog or the cry of the jackal that kept him awake, or the persistent questioning; but a premonition of crisis and of an end to something.

Chapter Twenty

The postman brought a letter from Somi.

Dear Rusty, best favourite friend,

Do not ever travel in a third-class compartment. All the way to Amritsar I had to sleep standing up, the carriage was so crowded.

I shall be coming back to Dehra in the spring, in time to watch you play Holi with Ranbir. I know you feel like leaving India and running off to England, but wait until you see me again, all right? You are afraid to die without having done something. You are afraid to die, Rusty, but you have hardly begun to live.

I know you are not happy in Dehra, and you must be lonely. But wait a little, be patient, and the bad days will pass. We don't know why we live. It is no use trying to know. But we have to live, Rusty, because we really want to. And as long as we want to, we have got to find something to live for, and even die for it. Mother is keeping well and sends you her greetings. Tell me whatever you need.

Somi

Rusty folded the letter carefully, and put it in his shirt pocket; he meant to keep it forever. He could not wait for Somi's return; but he knew that their friendship would last a lifetime, and that the beauty of it would always be with him. In and out of Rusty's life, his turban at an angle, Somi would go, his slippers slapping against his heels forever . . .

Rusty had no case or bedding roll to pack, no belongings at all; only the clothes he wore, which were Somi's, and about fifty rupees, for which he had to thank Kishen. He had made no preparations for the journey; he would slip away without fuss or bother; insignificant, unnoticed . . .

An hour before leaving for the station, he lay down to rest. He gazed up at the ceiling, where the lizards scuttled about: callous creatures, unconcerned with his departure: one human was just the same as any other. And the bald maina, hopping on and off the window sill, would continue to fight and lose more feathers; and the crows and the squirrels in the mango tree, they would be missed by

Rusty, but they would not miss him. It was true, one human was no different to any other – except to a dog or a human . . .

When Rusty left the room, there was activity at the water tank; clothes were being beaten on the stone, and the ayah's trinkets were jingling away. Rusty couldn't bear to say goodbye to the people at the water tank, so he didn't close his door, lest they suspect him of leaving. He descended the steps – twenty-two of them, he counted for the last time – and crossed the drain, and walked slowly down the gravel path until he was out of the compound.

He crossed the maidan, where a group of students were playing cricket, whilst another group wrestled; prams were wheeled in and out of the sporting youths; young girls gossiped away the morning. And Rusty remembered his first night on the maidan, when he had been frightened and wet and lonely; and now, though the maidan was crowded, he felt the same loneliness, the same isolation. In the bazaar, he walked with a heavy heart. From the chaat shop came the familiar smell of spices and the crackle of frying fat. And the children bumped him, and the cows blocked the road; and, though he knew they always did these things, it was only now that he noticed them. They all seemed to be holding him, pulling him back.

But he could not return; he was afraid of what lay ahead, he dreaded the unknown, but it was easier to walk forwards than backwards.

The toy seller made his way through the crowd, children clustering round him, tearing at his pole. Rusty fingered a two-anna piece, and his eye picked out a little plume of red feathers, that seemed to have no useful purpose, and he was determined to buy it.

But before he could make the purchase, someone plucked at his shirt sleeve.

'Chotta sahib, chotta sahib,' said the sweeper boy, Mr Harrison's servant.

Rusty could not mistake the shaved head and the sparkle of white teeth, and wanted to turn away; ignore the sweeper boy, who was linked up with a past that was distant and yet uncomfortably close. But the hand plucked at his sleeve, and Rusty felt ashamed, angry with himself for trying to ignore someone who had never harmed him and who couldn't have been friendlier. Rusty was a sahib no longer, no one was his servant; and he was not an Indian, he had no caste, he could not call another untouchable . . .

. . . 'You are not at work?' asked Rusty.

'No work.' The sweeper boy smiled, a flash of white in the darkness of his face.

'What of Mr Harrison, the sahib?'

'Gone.'

'Gone,' said Rusty, and was surprised at not being surprised. 'Where has he gone?'

'Don't know, but he gone for good. Before he go, I get sack. I drop the bathroom water on veranda, and the sahib, he hit me on the head with his hand, *put!* . . . I say, sahib, you are cruel, and he say, cruelty to animals, no? Then he tell me I get sack, he leaving anyway. I lose two days' pay.'

Rusty was filled with both relief and uncertainty, and for the same reason; now there could never be a return; whether he wanted to or not, he could never go back to his old home.

'What about the others?' asked Rusty.

'They still there. Missionary's wife a fine lady, she give me five rupees before I go.'

'And you? You are working now?'

Again the sweeper boy flashed his smile. 'No work . . .'

Rusty didn't dare offer the boy any money, though it would probably have been accepted; in the sweeper boy he saw nobility, and he could not belittle nobility.

'I will try to get you work,' he said, forgetting that he was on his way to the station to buy a one-way ticket, and telling the sweeper boy where he lived.

Instinctively, the sweeper boy did not believe him; he nodded his head automatically, but his eyes signified disbelief; and when Rusty left him, he was still nodding; and to nobody in particular.

On the station platform the coolies pushed and struggled, shouted incomprehensibly, lifted heavy trunks with apparent ease. Merchants cried their wares, trundling barrows up and down the platform: soda water, oranges, betel nut, *halwai* sweets . . . The flies swarmed around the open stalls, clustered on glass-covered sweet boxes; the mongrel dogs, ownerless and unfed, roved the platform and railway lines, hunting for scraps of food and stealing at every opportunity.

Ignoring Somi's advice, Rusty bought a third-class ticket and found an empty compartment. The guard blew his whistle, but nobody took any notice. People continued about their business, certain that the train wouldn't start for another ten minutes: the Hardwar Mail never did start on time.

Rusty was the only person in the compartment until a fat lady, complaining volubly, oozed in through the door and spread herself across an entire bunk; her plan, it seemed, was to discourage other passengers from coming in. She had beady little eyes, set in a big moon face; and they looked at Rusty in curiosity, darting away whenever they met with his.

Others came in, in quick succession now, for the guard had blown his whistle a second time: a young woman with a baby, a soldier in uniform, a boy of about twelve . . . they were all poor people; except for the fat lady, who travelled third class in order to save money.

The guard's whistle blew again, but the train still refused to start. Being the Hardwar Mail, this was but natural; no one ever expected the Hardwar Mail to start on time, for in all its history, it hadn't done so (not even during the time of the British), and for it to do so now would be a blow to tradition. Everyone was for tradition, and so the Hardwar Mail was not permitted to arrive and depart at the appointed hour; though it was feared that one day some young fool would change the appointed hours. And imagine what would happen if the train did leave on time – the entire railway system would be thrown into confusion for, needless to say, every other train took its time from the Hardwar Mail . . .

So the guard kept blowing his whistle, and the vendors put their heads in at the windows, selling oranges and newspapers and soda water . . .

'Soda water!' exclaimed the fat lady. 'Who wants soda water! Why, our farmer here has with him a *sohrai* of pure cool water, and he will share it with us, will he not? Paan-wallah! Call the man, quick, he is not even stopping at the window!'

The guard blew his whistle again. And they were off.

The Hardwar Mail, true to tradition, pulled out of Dehra station half an hour late.

Perhaps it was because Rusty was leaving Dehra forever that he took an unusual interest in everything he saw and heard. Things that would not normally have been noticed by him now made vivid impressions on his mind: the gesticulations of the coolies as the train drew out of the station, a dog licking a banana skin, a naked child alone amongst a pile of bundles, crying its heart out . . .

. . . The platform, fruit stalls, advertisement boards, all slipped away.

The train gathered speed, the carriages groaned and creaked and rocked crazily. But, as they left the town and the station behind, the wheels found their rhythm, beating time with the rails and singing a song.

It was a sad song, persistent and fatalistic. Another life was finishing.

One morning, months ago, Rusty had heard a drum in the forest, a single drum-beat, *dhum-tap*; and in the stillness of the morning it had been a call, a message, an irresistible force. He had cut away from his roots: he had been replanted, had sprung to life, new life. But it was too quick a growth, rootless, and he had withered. And now he had run away again. No drum now; instead, the pulsating throb and tremor of the train rushing him away; away from India, from Somi, from the chaat shop and the bazaar; and he did not know why, except that he was lost and lonely and tired and old: nearly seventeen, but old . . .

The little boy beside him knelt in front of the window, and counted the telegraph posts as they flashed by; they seemed, after a while, to be hurtling past whilst the train stood stationary. Only the rocking of the carriage could be felt.

The train sang through the forests, and sometimes the child waved his hand excitedly and pointed out a deer, the sturdy sambar or delicate cheetal. Monkeys screamed from treetops, or loped beside the train, mothers with their young clinging to their breasts. The jungle was heavy, shutting off the sky, and it was like this for half an hour; then the train came into the open, and the sun struck through the carriage windows. They swung through cultivated land, maize and sugar cane fields; past squat, mud-hut villages, and teams of bullocks ploughing up the soil; leaving behind only a trail of curling smoke.

Children ran out from the villages – brown, naked children – and waved to the train, crying words of greeting; and the little boy in the compartment waved back and shouted merrily, and then turned to look at his travelling companions, his eyes shining with pleasure. The child began to chatter about this and that, and the others listened to him good-humouredly; the farmer with simplicity and a genuine interest, the fat lady with a tolerant smile, and the soldier with an air of condescension. The young woman and the baby were both asleep. Rusty felt sleepy himself, and was unable to listen to the small boy; vaguely, he thought of Kishen, and of how surprised and pleased Kishen would be to see him.

Presently he fell asleep.

When he awoke, the train was nearing Hardwar; he had slept for almost an hour, but to him it seemed like five minutes.

His throat was dry and, though his shirt was soaked with perspiration, he shivered a little. His hands trembled, and he had to close his fists to stop the trembling.

At midday the train steamed into Hardwar station, and disgorged its passengers.

The fat lady, who was determined to be the first out of the compartment, jammed the doorway; but Rusty and the soldier outwitted her by climbing out of the window.

Rusty felt better once he was outside the station, but he knew he had a fever. The rocking of the train continued, and the song of the wheels and the rails kept beating in his head. He walked slowly away from the station, comforted by the thought that at Kishen's aunt's house there would be food and rest. At night, he would catch the Delhi train.

Chapter Twenty-one

The house was on top of a hill, and from the road Rusty could see the river below, and the temples, and hundreds of people moving about on the long graceful steps that sloped down to the water: for the river was holy, and Hardwar sacred, a place of pilgrimage.

He knocked on the door, and presently there was the sound of bare feet on a stone floor. The door was opened by a lady, but she was a stranger to Rusty, and they looked at each other with puzzled, questioning eyes.

'Oh . . . namaste ji,' faltered Rusty. 'Does – does Kapoor or his sister live here?'

The lady of the house did not answer immediately. She looked at the boy with a detached interest, trying to guess at his business and intentions. She was dressed simply and well, she had a look of refinement, and Rusty felt sure that her examination of him was no more than natural curiosity.

'Who are you, please?' she asked.

'I am a friend from Dehra. I am leaving India and I want to see Kapoor and his son before I go. Are they here?'

'Only Kapoor is here,' she said. 'You can come in.'

Rusty wondered where Kishen and his aunt could be, but he did not want to ask this strange lady; he felt ill at ease in her presence; the house seemed to be hers. Coming straight into the front room from bright sunshine, his eyes took a little time to get used to the dark; but after a moment or two he made out the form of Kapoor, sitting in a cushioned armchair.

'Hullo, Mister Rusty,' said Kapoor. 'It is nice to see you.'

There was a glass of whisky on the table, but Kapoor was not drunk; he was shaved and dressed, and looked a good deal younger than when Rusty had last seen him. But something else was missing. His jovial friendliness, his enthusiasm, had gone. This Kapoor was a different man to the Kapoor of the beard and green dressing gown.

'Hullo, Mister Kapoor,' said Rusty. 'How are you?'

'I am fine, just fine. Sit down, please. Will you have a drink?'

'No thanks. I came to see you and Kishen before leaving for England. I wanted to see you again, you were very kind to me . . .'

'That's all right, quite all right. I'm very glad to see you, but I'm afraid Kishen isn't here. By the way, the lady who just met you at the door, I haven't introduced you yet – this is my wife, Mister Rusty . . . I – I married again shortly after Meena's death.'

Rusty looked at the new Mrs Kapoor in considerable bewilderment, and greeted her quietly. It was not unusual for a man to marry again soon after his wife's death, and he knew it, but his heart was breaking with a fierce anger. He was revolted by the rapidity of it all; hardly a month had passed, and here was Kapoor with another wife. Rusty remembered that it was for this man Kapoor – this weakling, this drunkard, this self-opinionated, selfish drunkard – that Meena had given her life, all of it; devotedly she had remained by his side when she could have left, when there was no more fight in him and no more love in him and no more pride in him; and, had she left then, she would be alive, and he – *he* would be dead . . .

Rusty was not interested in the new Mrs Kapoor. For Kapoor, he had only contempt.

'Mister Rusty is a good friend of the family,' Kapoor was saying. 'In Dehra he was a great help to Kishen.'

'How did Meena die?' asked Rusty, determined to hurt Kapoor – if Kapoor could be hurt . . .

'I thought you knew. We had an accident. Let us not talk of it, Mister Rusty . . .'

'The driver was driving, of course?'

Kapoor did not answer immediately, but raised his glass and sipped from it.

'Of course,' he said.

'How did it all happen?'

'Please, Mister Rusty, I do not want to describe it. We were going too fast, and the car left the road and hit a tree. I can't describe it, Mister Rusty.'

'No, of course not,' said Rusty. 'Anyway, I am glad nothing happened to you. It is also good that you have mastered your natural grief, and started a new life. I am afraid I am not as strong as you. Meena was wonderful, and I still can't believe she is dead.'

'We have to carry on . . .'

'Of course. How is Kishen? I would like to see him.'

'He is in Lucknow with his aunt,' said Kapoor. 'He wished to stay with her.'

Mrs Kapoor had been quiet till now.

'Tell him the truth,' she said. 'There is nothing to hide.'

'You tell him then.'

'What do you mean?'

'He ran away from us. As soon as his aunt left, he ran away. We tried to make him come back, but it was useless, so now we don't try. But he is in Hardwar. We are always hearing about him. They say he is the most cunning thief on both sides of the river.'

'Where can I find him?'

'I don't know. He is wanted by the police. He robs for others, and they pay him. It is easier for a young boy to steal than it is for a man, and as he is quite a genius at it, his services are in demand. And I am sure he would not hesitate to rob us too . . .'

'But you must know where I can find him,' persisted Rusty. 'You must have some idea.'

'He has been seen along the river and in the bazaar. I don't know where he lives. In a tree, perhaps, or in a temple, or in a brothel. He is somewhere in Hardwar, but exactly where I do not know . . . no one knows. He speaks to no one and runs from everyone. What can you want with him?'

'He is my friend,' said Rusty.

'He will rob you too.'

'The money I have is what he gave me.'

He rose to leave; he was tired, but he did not want to stay much longer in this alien house.

'You are tired,' said Mrs Kapoor. 'Will you rest, and have your meal with us?'

'No,' said Rusty, 'there isn't time.'

Chapter Twenty-two

All hope left Rusty as he staggered down the hill, weak and exhausted. He could not think clearly; he knew he hadn't eaten since morning, and cursed himself for not accepting Mrs Kapoor's hospitality.

He was hungry, he was thirsty; he was tormented by thoughts of what might have happened to Kishen, of what might happen . . .

He stumbled down the long steps that led to the water. The sun was strong, striking up from the stone and shimmering against the great white temple that overlooked the river. He crossed the courtyard and came to the water's edge.

Lying on his belly on the riverbank, he drank of the holy waters. Then he pulled off his shirt and sandals, and slipped into the water. There were men and women on all sides, praying with their faces to the sun. Great fish swam round them, unafraid and unmolested, safe in the sacred waters of the Ganges.

When he had bathed and refreshed himself, Rusty climbed back on to the stone bank. His sandals and shirt had disappeared.

No one was near except a beggar leaning on a stick, a young man massaging his body with oils, and a cow examining an empty, discarded basket; and, of the three, the cow was the most likely suspect; it had probably eaten the sandals.

But Rusty no longer cared what happened to his things. His money was in the leather purse attached to his belt; and, as long as he had the belt, he had both money and pyjamas.

He rolled the wet pyjamas up to his thighs; then, staring ahead with unseeing eyes, ignoring the bowls that were thrust before him by the beggars, he walked the length of the courtyard that ran parallel to the rising steps.

Children were shouting at each other, priests chanting their prayers; vendors, with baskets on their heads – baskets of fruit and chaat – gave harsh cries; and the cows pushed their way around at will. Steps descended from all parts of the hill; broad, clean steps from the temple, and narrow, winding steps from the bazaars; and a maze of alleyways zigzagged about the hill, through the bazaar, round the temples, along the river, and were lost amongst themselves and found again and lost . . .

Kishen, barefooted and ragged and thin, but with the same supreme confidence in himself, leant against the wall of an alleyway, and watched Rusty's progress along the riverbank.

He wanted to shout to Rusty, to go to him, to embrace him, but he could not do these things. He did not understand the reason for his friend's presence, he could not reveal himself for fear of a trap. He was sure it was Rusty he watched, for who else was there with the same coloured hair and skin who would walk half-naked in Hardwar? It was Rusty, but why . . . was he in trouble, was he sick? Why, why . . . ?

Rusty saw Kishen in the alleyway. He was too weak to shout. He stood in the sun, and looked up the steps at Kishen standing in the alleyway.

Kishen did not know whether to run to Rusty, or run away. He, too, stood still, at the entrance of the alley.

'Hullo, Rusty,' he called.

And Rusty began to walk up the steps, slowly and painfully, his feet burning, his head reeling, his heart thundering with conflicting emotions.

'Are you alone?' called Kishen. 'Don't come if you are not alone.'

Rusty advanced up the steps, until he was in the alley-way facing Kishen. Despite the haze before his eyes, he noticed Kishen's wild condition; the bones protruded from the boy's skin, his hair was knotted and straggly, his eyes danced, searching the steps for others.

'Why are you here, Rusty?'

'To see you . . .'

'Why?'

'I am going away.'

'How can you go anywhere? You look sick enough to die.'

'I came to see you, anyway.'

'Why?'

Rusty sat down on a step; his wrists hung loose on his knees, and his head drooped forward.

'I'm hungry,' he said.

Kishen walked into the open, and approached a fruit vendor.

He came back with two large watermelons.

'You have money?' asked Rusty.

'No. Just credit. I bring them profits, they give me credit.'

He sat down beside Rusty, produced a small but wicked-looking knife from the folds of his shirt, and proceeded to slice the melons in half.

'You can't go away,' he said.

'I can't go back.'

'Why not?'

'No money, no job, no friends.'

They put their teeth into the watermelon, and ate at terrific speed. Rusty felt much refreshed; he put his weakness and fever down to an empty stomach.

'I'll be no good as a bandit,' said Rusty. 'I can be recognized at sight, I can't go round robbing people, I don't think it's very nice anyway.'

'I don't rob poor people,' objected Kishen, prodding his nose. 'I only rob those who've got something to be robbed. And I don't do it for myself, that's why I'm never caught. People pay me to do their dirty work. Like that, they are safe because they are somewhere else when everything happens, and I am safe because I don't have what I rob, and haven't got a reason for taking it anyway . . . so it is quite safe. But don't worry, bhai, we will not do it in Dehra, we are too well-known there. Besides, I am tired of running from the police.'

'Then what will we do?'

'Oh, we will find someone for you to give English lessons. Not one, but many. And I will start a chaat shop.'

'When do we go?' said Rusty; and England and fame and riches were all forgotten, and would soon be dreams again.

'Tomorrow morning, early,' said Kishen. 'There is a boat crossing the river. We must cross the river, on this side I am known, and there are many people who would not like me to leave. If we went by train, I would be caught at the station, for sure. On the other side no one knows me, there is only jungle.'

Rusty was amazed at how competent and practical Kishen had become; Kishen's mind had developed far quicker than his body, and he was a funny cross between an experienced adventurer and a ragged urchin. A month ago he had clung to Rusty for protection; now Rusty looked to Kishen for guidance.

I wonder, thought Rusty, *will they notice my absence in Dehra? After all, I have only been away a day, though it seems an age . . . the room on the roof will still be vacant when I return, no one but me could be crazy enough to live in such a room . . . I will go back to the room as though nothing had happened, and no one will notice that anything has.*

★

The afternoon ripened into evening.

As the sun sank, the temple changed from white to gold, from gold to orange, from orange to pink, and from pink to crimson, and all these colours were in turn reflected in the surrounding waters.

The noise subsided gradually, the night came on.

Kishen and Rusty slept in the open, on the temple steps. It was a warm night, the air was close and heavy. In the shadows lay small bundles of humanity, the roofless and the homeless, sleeping only to pass the time of night. Rusty slept in spasms, waking frequently with a nagging pain in his stomach; poor stomach, it couldn't stand the unfamiliar strain of emptiness.

Chapter Twenty-three

Before the steps and the riverbank came to life, Kishen and Rusty climbed into the ferry boat. It would be crossing the river all day, carrying pilgrims from temple to temple, charging nothing. And though it was very early, and this the first crossing, a free passage across the river made for a crowded boat.

The people who climbed in were even more diverse than those Rusty had met on the train: women and children, bearded old men and wrinkled women, strong young peasants – not the prosperous or mercantile class, but the poor – who had come miles, mostly on foot, to bathe in the sacred waters of the Ganges.

On shore, the steps began to come to life. The previous day's cries and prayers and rites were resumed with the same monotonous devotion, at the same pitch, in the same spirit of timelessness; and the steps sounded to the tread of many feet, sandalled, slippered and bare.

The boat floated low in the water, it was so heavy, and the oarsmen had to strain upstream in order to avoid being swept down by the current. Their muscles shone and rippled under the grey iron of their weather-beaten skins. The blades of the oars cut through the water, in and out; and between grunts, the oarsmen shouted the time of the stroke.

Kishen and Rusty sat crushed together in the middle of the boat. There was no likelihood of their being separated now, but they held hands.

The people in the boat began to sing.

It was a low hum at first, but someone broke in with a song, and the voice – a young voice, clear and pure – reminded Rusty of Somi; and he comforted himself with the thought that Somi would be back in Dehra in the spring.

They sang in time to the stroke of the oars, in and out, and the grunts and shouts of the oarsmen throbbed their way into the song, becoming part of it.

An old woman, who had white hair and a face lined with deep ruts, said: 'It is beautiful to hear the children sing.'

'Then you too should sing,' said Rusty.

She smiled at him, a sweet, toothless smile.

'What are you, my son, are you one of us? I have never, on this river, seen blue eyes and golden hair.'

'I am nothing,' said Rusty. 'I am everything.' He stated it bluntly, proudly.

'Where is your home, then?'

'I have no home,' he said, and felt proud of that too.

'And who is the boy with you?' asked the old woman, a genuine busybody. 'What is he to you?'

Rusty did not answer; he was asking himself the same question: what was Kishen to him? He was sure of one thing, they were both refugees – refugees from the world . . . They were each other's shelter, each other's refuge, each other's help. Kishen was a *jungli*, divorced from the rest of mankind, and Rusty was the only one who understood him – because Rusty too was divorced from mankind. And theirs was a tie that would hold, because they were the only people who knew each other and loved each other.

Because of this tie, Rusty had to go back. And it was with relief that he went back. His return was justified.

He let his hand trail over the side of the boat: he wanted to remember the touch of the water as it moved past them, down and away: it would come to the ocean, the ocean that was life.

He could not run away. He could not escape the life he had made, the ocean into which he had floundered the night he left his guardian's house. He had to return to the room, *his* room; he had to go back.

The song died away as the boat came ashore. They disembarked, walking over the smooth pebbles; and the forest rose from the edge of the river, and beckoned them.

Rusty remembered the forest on the day of the picnic, when he had kissed Meena and held her hands, and he remembered the magic of the forest and the magic of Meena.

'One day,' he said, 'we must live in the jungle.'

'One day,' said Kishen, and he laughed. 'But now we walk back. We walk back to the room on the roof! It is our room, we have to go back!'

They had to go back: to bathe at the water tank and listen to the morning gossip, to sit in the fruit trees and eat in the chaat shop and perhaps make a garden on the roof; to eat and sleep; to work; to live; to die.

Kishen laughed.

'One day you'll be great, Rusty. A writer or an actor or a prime minister or something. Maybe a poet! Why not a poet, Rusty?'

Rusty smiled. He knew he was smiling, because he was smiling at himself.

'Yes,' he said, 'why not a poet?'

So they began to walk.

Ahead of them lay forest and silence – and what was left of time . . .

THE ORIGINALS
Iconic • Outspoken • First

💡 FOR THINKERS

- [ ] **Dear Nobody**
  Berlie Doherty

- [ ] **Buddy**
  Nigel Hinton

- [ ] **The Red Pony**
  John Steinbeck

- [ ] **The Wave**
  Morton Rhue

♡ FOR LOVERS

- [ ] **I Capture the Castle**
  Dodie Smith

- [ ] **Across the Barricades**
  Joan Lingard

- [ ] **The Twelfth Day of July**
  Joan Lingard

- [ ] **Postcards from No Man's Land**
  Aidan Chambers

✊ FOR REBELS

- [ ] **The Outsiders**
  S. E. Hinton

- [ ] **The Pearl**
  John Steinbeck

- [ ] **No Turning Back**
  Beverley Naidoo

☢ FOR SURVIVORS

- [ ] **Z for Zachariah**
  Richard C. O'Brien

- [ ] **After the First Death**
  Robert Cormier

- [ ] **Stone Cold**
  Robert Swindells

- [ ] **The Endless Steppe**
  Esther Hautzig

What are you reading? Tell *@penguinplatform #OriginalYA*

YouTube

6 BOOKS TO MAKE YOU THINK

...AND CRY AND THINK AGAIN

THE ORIGINALS

DEAR NOBODY
by Berlie Doherty

Helen writes tender letters to her unplanned unborn baby.

THE RED PONY
by John Steinbeck

A celebration of a blessed but sometimes brutal adolescence in rural California.

BUDDY
by Nigel Hinton

Buddy's father has always lived on the edges of the criminal underworld, but things just got serious.

ALL THE BRIGHT PLACES
by Jennifer Niven

Violet is a girl who learns to live from a boy who wants to die.

THE ONE MEMORY OF FLORA BANKS
by Emily Barr

You always remember your first kiss – Flora remembers nothing else.

BOYS DON'T CRY
by Malorie Blackman

Dante Bridgeman didn't expect to be left holding the baby.

Thinkers follow: **#OriginalYA**

LOVE AGAINST THE ODDS . . .

THE ORIGINALS

. . . in genteel poverty

. . . in Belfast during the Troubles

. . . across a religious divide

. . . in occupied England

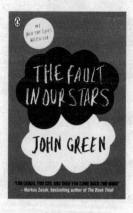

. . . in a cancer support group

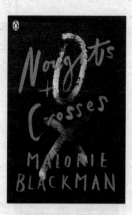

. . . in a segregated society

What's your story?  #OriginalYA

REBEL STORIES

THE ORIGINALS

REBEL: **Pony Boy Curtis**, *Greaser*

SKILL: *Writing (he penned* THE ORIGINAL *teenage rebel story)*

CAUSE: *Protecting his friend after a fight with rival gang, the Socs, leads to a fatal knifing*

REBEL: **Sipho**, *a young South African runaway*

SKILL: Bravery

CAUSE: *Surviving on the cut-throat streets of post-apartheid South Africa*

REBEL: **Kino**, *a Mexican pearl diver and dedicated father*

SKILL: *Possesses a precious pearl that is coveted by all*

CAUSE: *Overcoming the prejudice that endangers his son's life*

Whose side are you on?   *#OriginalYA*

REBEL: **Nathan**, *Half Code and son of the world's most feared black witch*

SKILLS: Strength and fortitude

CAUSE: *To find his father, Marcus, and receive the three gifts that will confirm him as a fully-fledged witch – before his seventeenth birthday*

REBEL: **Gemma**, *anarchist and addict*

SKILL: Troublemaking

CAUSE: *Saving Tar, her first love, from his abusive father and doing anything to get her next hit*

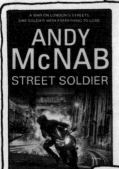

REBEL: **Sean Harker**, *soldier*

SKILLS: Stealing cars and fighting

CAUSE: *He's turned his life around and now he must put his street skills to the ultimate test: as a soldier in the British army*

REBEL: **Lada Dracul**, *ruthless anti-princess and brutal military leader in the Ottoman Court*

SKILLS: Wielding a dagger and defying gender convention

CAUSE: *To become the prince and vaivode of her homeland, Wallachia*

He just wanted a decent book to read ...

Not too much to ask, is it? It was in 1935 when Allen Lane, Managing Director of Bodley Head Publishers, stood on a platform at Exeter railway station looking for something good to read on his journey back to London. His choice was limited to popular magazines and poor-quality paperbacks – the same choice faced every day by the vast majority of readers, few of whom could afford hardbacks. Lane's disappointment and subsequent anger at the range of books generally available led him to found a company – and change the world.

'We believed in the existence in this country of a vast reading public for intelligent books at a low price, and staked everything on it'
Sir Allen Lane, 1902–1970, founder of Penguin Books

The quality paperback had arrived – and not just in bookshops. Lane was adamant that his Penguins should appear in chain stores and tobacconists, and should cost no more than a packet of cigarettes.

Reading habits (and cigarette prices) have changed since 1935, but Penguin still believes in publishing the best books for everybody to enjoy. We still believe that good design costs no more than bad design, and we still believe that quality books published passionately and responsibly make the world a better place.

So wherever you see the little bird – whether it's on a piece of prize-winning literary fiction or a celebrity autobiography, political tour de force or historical masterpiece, a serial-killer thriller, reference book, world classic or a piece of pure escapism – you can bet that it represents the very best that the genre has to offer.

Whatever you like to read – trust Penguin.